AF185015

Yelina Angehrn

The last Werewolves

After the fight

## About the Autor

Yelina Angehrn was born in Wil (Switzerland) on 8 November 2007. Yelina is the oldest of two sisters growing in the swiss countryside. As daughter of a swiss mother and a Swiss-Venezuelan father with an English/Spanish speaking background, which influenced Yelina to write in English. While writing is Yelinas passion and main interest she still goes to local secondary school. Her interest in fantasy was awaken by the stories her dad will invent every night for her and her little sister.

Her other passion is the world of wolves and big cats. Which is reflected in her stories.

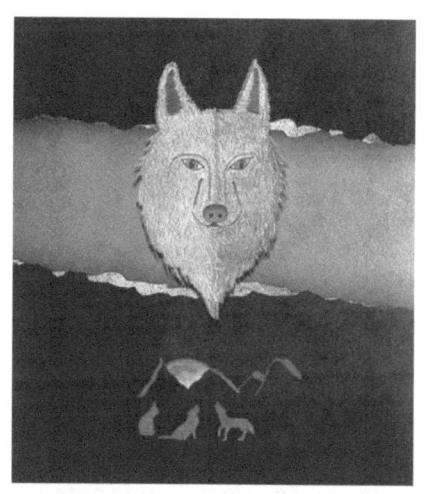

# The last
# Werewolves

After the fight

Copyright © 2021 Yelina E. Angehrn
Cover, Illustration: Andrea T. Angehrn

Publisher & Print:      tredition GmbH
                        Halenreie 40-44
                        22359 Hamburg

Paperback       ISBN: 978-3-347-23183-2
e-Book          ISBN: 978-3-347-23185-6

The German National Library records this publication in the German National Bibliographic; detailed bibliographic information is provided via the following link:
http://dnb.ddb.de

# Characters

# Werewolves

Achak: Young werewolf boy with night black, curly hair that reach him to the chin, and brown eyes. As a werewolf he has got black fur and brown-yellow eyes that mostly shine in a bright amber-golden color. His name means Spirit.

Annawan: Werewolf man with short, black hair and brown eyes. As a werewolf he has got light-brown fur and orange-red eyes. His name means Chief.

# Shapeshifters

Adahy: Jong shapeshifter with brown hair and orange-brown eyes. He transforms into a Lynx.

Adam: Jong shapeshifter with brown hair with some grey and blue eyes. He takes the form of a wolf with grey and brown fur.

Dexter: 13 years old Shapeshifter with fire red hair and sand- brown eyes. He takes the form of a red fox.

Chatan: Shapeshifter with grey hair and yellow eyes. He takes the form of a peregrine falcon.

Kai: Shapeshifter with brown hair and blue eyes. He transforms into a red fox.

Steffi and Steve: Shapeshifter twins with nut-brown hair and eyes. They both take the form of squirrels.

# Witches/Wizards

Karl: Jong wizard boy with short, black hair and black eyes.

Alaika: Witch with long blond hair and blue eyes.

Jack: Wizard with white- blond hair and blue eyes.

# Prolog

The full moon just set, and the sun rose while shining on the dark mountains. In the forest stood a werewolf with black fur and yellow-brown eyes. Just as the sun shone on his fur, he began to howl in pain, while transforming into a human boy with curly and black hair which reached down to the chin and with brown eyes. His arms were bleeding, his legs and even his face. Achak the wild one looked around in confusion, where was he? Then, suddenly all the memories of the last night flashed like pictures in his head. Just as the full moon shone on him and then there was a bang and humans appeared, they had guns and were shooting on him, his sister and his fellow packmates. A few shots also hit him in face, legs, arms and back, but not as badly as they hit Mai, his twin sister, his big brothers Tokala and Hakan, his parents Tocho and Tala. He knew it was hopeless to wait for them, Achak knew his mother Tala and his father Tocho were dead, but he hoped that at least his sister Mai survived. Hakan had had no chance of surviving after all, he blocked a shot which should have hit Achak... and died. And while Tokala was protecting the pups... he got shot right in the chest. Achak was filled with pain as he remembered and thought about it. But he could not remember that his sister was hurt deadly, and hope grew within him. Could it be that Mai was still alive? If it were so he had to find her and that had to happen quickly, or the hunters could find her before he does! He could not let that happen! Achak tried to transform into his black-haired wolf-me. Under a painful howl he transformed and began to walk to his lair to search for clues where his sister could be.

When he arrived, he immediately searched the ground with his fine nose. The ground was full of blood, fur, footprints of humans and prints of werewolves. He saw bodies of his fellow packmates and as he saw the dead body of a white female wolf with brown ears, Achak howled painfully at the sight of his mother. But he noticed that not all his mates were there, he searched for Hakan but could not find him and he knew; the hunters must have taken the bodies to take their fur. Achak searched again and finally found the footprints of Mai, he recognized them because Mai limped. He followed them and hoped he would find his sister still alive.

# Chapter 1

"I give up!" Achak yelled. "I'll never find her!" "What makes you think that?", a lynx asked. Achak looked at him and answered furiously, "Because I've been searching for four moons, I can't take it anymore. I searched our whole territory, I searched the valley of death, the prairie, the Coyote forest, and the entire mountains. And I still haven't found her! I guess I just have to accept that she's dead!", he added sadly. The lynx looked at the frustrated, sad boy with black hair. "If I were you, I would also search the Human village." "What? Are you mad? I can't do that!" "Why not? I thought you were a werewolf. So, you could just search for her as a boy." "I don't think Mai would...", no wait. Mai was a huge fan of risks. No risk, no fun, she always said. "Well, I guess it's worth trying, right?" The lynx nodded and Achak took a deep breath. He would go to a human village... no big deal, after all, if they find out they would probably kill him, but no big deal. As Achak walked towards the village he began to sweat, his head, his feat, every muscle in his body commanded he should just turn around and run back into the forest where he came from.

A whole year had passed, Achak lived on the street but it wasn't really different to his life in the mountains, with his pack, now when he was hungry, he could just hunt a few mice or go to the forest and hunt a deer, a stag or a bird. His wounds hadn't really healed, so he was often bleeding and incapable of hunting for a few days till the wound stopped bleeding. Achak never saw a sign of his sister. One day as he was walking down the street and searching for his sister and food, another boy came towards him with three other boys next to him, Achak knew that this meant nothing good. The front boy, the alpha it seemed, stepped forward. "Well, well the little street dog." He raised his fist while two other boys came from behind, which Achak did not notice, grabbed him so the alpha boy could punch him in the stomach. "What are you going to do? Call your mother? Or your father?" He punched Achak in the face, which did not hurt as much as the words about his parents. "Where are they? Did they abandon you?" The big boy punched him in the nose. "Or were they killed? Or couldn't they tell the difference between you and the worthless street dogs?" He punched Achak so hard in the nose that Achak collapsed. The boys left while Achak forced himself to his feet and walked to the forest, sat on a big rock, transformed into a wolf, and began to howl. But he did not just howl, he began to sing. He was singing in pain, he was missing his sister and his pack, the pain was like a sharp claw ripping his soul. Claws ripping and scratching each memory, and each feeling for his pack out of

*Where are you? Please answer me,*

*Tell me, what should I do? How should I find you? Please answer me!*

*I don't know how I should find you! How I could be free.*

*You all left me! Tell me, what can I do?*

*I'm a soldier but it seems like I must give up the fight.*

*I can't escape, the string around my neck is too tight.*

*I don't know what I should do,*

*Without you!*

*Oh, please tell me what shall I do!*

*Please, just give me a clue,*

*Where to find you! What to do!*

*please, I've got nothing left, just an empty heart,*

*I need you sis; in my life you are a big part.*

*Please give me a sign, a clue...*

*Where are you? Where are you? Oh, where are you?*

Achak sang for a while, his song echoed in the mountains and the village. You could hear it through the whole forest and far over the village. After the sunset he stopped and went hunting. As he found a print of a wapiti, he followed it. Achak saw the wapiti on a clearing and sneaked up on it, as he was close enough to jump and kill it with one bite, he jumped and landed on the back of the wapiti. This was puma-hunting-style but since he didn't have his pack, he had to do it like this. He felt the blood of the animal on his tongue and looked in its eyes, so the spirit of the wapiti did not have to go alone to the great Horn. That was how wapitis, deer or stags called the one to welcome them to death. By wolves and coyotes, it was the moon Clan, for foxes the great zorro, for stags, deer or wapiti the great horn As the animal closed its eyes Achak ate every part that was left of the animal. Really everything! He turned back into a human boy and returned to the village. While walking towards the village he felt the pain of his over a year-old wounds and the new ones from the village boys. When he was in the village again, he wanted to find the boys and bite them, hurt them but then... suddenly he heard a voice, not just any voice... It was the voice of his dad. "Don't let anger guide you, Wild Spirit." And then, other voices joined, he heard the voice of his mother "Achak go, leave the village", then the deep, soft voice of his big brother Hakan: "Always remember; humans might be our enemies but never attack first." And then came the voice of Tokala "Be the clever fox, not the stupid human." Achak could hear the mockery in Tokalas voice, and his mother said again: "Achak, leave the village!", and then the voices fainted, they disappeared as fast as they had come. Achak remembered that voices of mates or wolves of old times only appeared if the one they are talking to was in great danger. "Wait a second, I can't be in danger", he said to himself. "After all there's nobody here." Achak sat on the hard concrete and was thinking that he had not heard the voice of his sister, that must mean that she was still alive! Achak wanted to jump and sing again but just in that moment the boys from before came again, but they had not seen him yet and Achak wasn't really keen on the thought that they'd see him again and beat him up. So, he turned and ran back to the forest, he wanted to transform in his wolf-form, but he saw a camera on a tree trunk. Achak knew that he could not transform because he could get flashed and so he could get caught. Of course, he knew a little bit of how to survive in human form, but he felt more comfortable as a wolf, after all he spent more time as a wolf as a human. He was 12 now and had spent almost seven hunting- seasons as a wolf, he knew how to make a bow and arrow, how to make clothes and how to make a fire. Achak knew if he would not go deeper into the forest the humans could find him. So, he walked deeper into the forest and searched for a lair. He found one, it was a badger's old home and now it would be his new one. He had to expand the hole and the lair itself. When he finished, he crawled into the lair to check if it was fitting for him, and it was. Meanwhile the sun was setting and Achak was hungry, so he searched for a stick that was long enough for a bow, and a second one for an arrow. As he found two twigs that matched what he was searching for he searched the ground for stones. It took a bit till he found stones, after all, he was in the forest. After he found a fitting stone, he took it to his lair and began to shape it in the form of an arrowhead and then he glued the arrowhead on the twig with birch pitch. He waited a while and watched the sunset, he thought of his mother and father, how his father showed him how to hunt, in wolf-form of course and how to control his temper a little bit. He thought of his parents for a long time, till he was sure that the birch pitch was dry. So now he had to attach the feathers that he found, it was not a perfect arrow, but it should do the trick. Now he only had to make the bow which was not tricky. It was already dark when he finished, so he had to hurry or otherwise all the prey would be gone. He could find a fresh footprint of a wild boar and one of a hares. In this case Achak went for the boar, because if he would hit it, he would have enough for the day and the next. Of course, he didn't really need to eat so much but you never know. He tracked the animal and as he saw it, he stretched the bow. Released. And... missed. Bloody snowstorm, almost, he thought. He went back to the lair after he searched the ground but couldn't find the arrow. He lay down in his lair and fell asleep. He dreamed of his parents, his brothers and his sister. He hadn't had such dreams for nearly a year, but because of the voices, his sorrow came over him like a great wave. He saw flashes of his earlier childhood, his father showing him how to hunt and track prey... His mother telling him and a girl with long, dark-brown hair and green eyes not to climb the ravine which was between the camp and the forest... him in a cave with a broken leg because he naturally ignored his mother ... He was nine and a big boy with sandy-blond hair showed him how to make a bow and an arrow... and then... he was eleven and the final fight of his pack was in full swing, he saw how Hakan took his final breath as he blocked a shot which should have hit Achak instead, how he was devastated at the look of his big brother which had the impression like he was sleeping.

Achak woke up bathed in sweat, tears ran over his cheeks, but he did not cry. He was sad, indeed, but he did not start to cry, for six years he had not cried. "I can't sleep anyway, best I'll go outside to find some stones and make weapons and tools", he muttered to himself. He went outside, the night was cool and Achak could smell the fresh air, could feel the cool wind, hear the little creek, an owl, and a rustle of the leaves. Achak thought of how Mai would have loved to wake up so early and roister with her brothers and chase some birds and squirrels, if they were in the forest. Great grief came over him as he thought of his sister, maybe she is dead and just couldn't say anything. Achak felt that it was no use to search longer for his sister. Over a year had passed when he was often in the village to search for Mai... and never found her. A wave of sorrow came over Achak once again. He went to search for stones for new arrows, for a spear, a knife and maybe a fishing rod. He found some good stones and some wood, he took everything to the lair and made some tools.


Achak was in the village once again but this time he wasn't searching for Mai till his eyes burned. One part of him was still hoping that Mai was alive, but his other part said no. Achak wanted to go to his lair and try to catch up on some sleep, but he didn't really come far. Three boys were standing right in front of him. They weren't really making a move to the side and they were making their fingers crack. Achak knew that this meant trouble and he wanted to turn around, but the alpha boy was standing right in front of Achak and he bumped into the big boy. "Well, well look who's back! Where were you, you little freak?" Achak didn't answer. Mighty snowstorm, what was a "freak"? He knew what they meant when they called him street dog, street rat or other kinds of insults, but they never called him "freak". Achak wanted to ask what a freak was but just as he opened his mouth to ask the alpha talked again. "Where were you? With your mummy, crying? Haha! Look he's really got tears in his eyes! Look!", he shouted to his mates. Achak wanted to transform so he could hurt the alpha, hurt him so badly so that he could not stand for the next three days! Achak could feel how some fur started to grow on his arms and how his backbone was getting longer and turned into a tail. Now! That could not happen! I am a *human, I am a human,* he thought, *a biped human... a biped which does not have any respect for animals!* Achak could not stop transforming! His teeth grew to long fangs. The boys did not seem to notice because they started hitting Achak in the stomach. He fell. The boys were laughing. Achak was overwhelmed by his instincts. His head grew longer into a black wolf snout. Now the boys noticed! The three boys looked terrified when they saw the young boy turning into a werewolf. They backed away from the werewolf. Damn! Why!? Why can't I just control myself? Why couldn't I just accidentally transform into a normal wolf? The boys wanted to run away, not a really good idea! The black werewolf with brown-yellow eyes could not stop himself. He attacked.

# Chapter 2

The werewolf attacked. The boy, which seemed to be the "beta", wanted to run left, right in front of Achak-the-werewolf was fast, though, the beta boy was quick too! Before Achak knew what he was doing, he was biting the beta boy already! As Achak noticed he released the boy immediately, but the alpha boy was now screaming for help and five grownup men were there and were shooting at Achak. Achak got a graze shot at the shoulder, the memories of the night a year ago overcame him, and the pain was suddenly more than just the shot. It felt like long fangs that were ripping the meat of his bones, like arrows that hit him right in the chest. He didn't want to fight, and yet he wanted. He wanted to pay the humans back what they did to him! But he couldn't, not now and... because he knew his sister would not have wanted that. So, Achak turned and fled to the forest.

Days passed since he transformed into a werewolf. As he reached the forest he transformed back into a human boy, not a moment too early! The humans were running beside him through the forest, searching for the beast which attacked their cubs. Or "children" like the humans say. Achak was afraid but he did not show, he did not even show to himself. *I am not afraid; I am not afraid! Why should I be?* But then he admitted to himself that he was afraid. *Mai, please if you can hear me, please give me a sign. I think I do need your help I... I am... I am afraid. I am afraid you are still alive, and I'll die if I'm not careful. I am afraid that other clans will die because of me, if the humans can kill me, they'll know that there are werewolves, and... I don't want that. Achak was not sure Mai heard him but it's always worth trying.* "Now I know what mom, dad and my brothers meant.", he mumbled. He really was in danger! Okay, stay calm. He sneaked away from the grown-up men, to his lair, he had to pack the most important things and then go! Hm, where should I go? ... Aha! I could go to the light mountains there should be another pack... even dough I have not heard anything of them since I was seven! Achak packed his spear, his bow and one arrow and some of the other tools he made: a knife, a dagger and some sticks. He had to hurry, he had to get out of his former territory. Then, suddenly he heard steps, and voices. *Oh, crap* he thought. How on earth did they get here so fast? *I've got to go!* Achak just wanted to sneak away as he heard the voices where to close, so he limped into his lair, and waited till the voices were gone. But that did not really go very fast, the humans were searching everywhere.

"Did you see him?" "Dad, I told you that freak boy, you know, the one with those curly black hair and brown eyes, turned into that werewolf... wolf ... that creature!" Achak felt anger as he looked outside and on the alpha boy, he was very big and had short blond hair, blue eyes and wore a white shirt and blue pants, and around his neck he had a necklace, but not just any necklace. It was a talon of a wolf, Achak crawled further to the entrance to make sure it was what he thought. No! Please no! he thought. The talon was not black like usually, it was white. Achak knew only one wolf or werewolf who had white talons. And that was Mai. Before Achak knew what, he was doing he jumped out of the lair, in wolf form. He jumped right at the boy, Achak wanted to bite him, hurt him, even kill him. How dare he wear that talon? Suddenly there was a shot. Achak yelled. He felt blood on his back. Holy full moon, one of the humans must have shot him in the back! Never mind, he said to himself, he had to disappear, now! But he could not, not without the talon of his sister. He snapped at the neck of the boy and ripped the necklace off him. With the necklace in his snout, he ran away, he was one of the fastest in his pack. And he was fast, though, wounded he was fast enough to get to his old home.

As he arrived, he wanted to go again, he could not bear to look at the bodies of his mates, his parents and his brothers. But he had to rest, he did not have a chance. He lay down, yelled, and jumped up again. His back was hurting badly. "Au!... Bloody hell I cannot sleep like this, besides, I won't get far with a sore back! I've got to wait; I'll travel to the light mountains... but only by night!" Achak was thinking, if he were already here, he could sing for his parents, brothers and mates.

*Hear the clapping of the little creek,*
*see the moon shine,*
*everything I seek,*
*is right behind an uncrossable line.*
*I lost my parents, my brothers,*
*I lost my sister too*
*I miss them more than all others,*
*you all were forced to go-o.*
*Oh Mai, I've searched for you,*
*a whole year without any clue*
*someone tell me... what should I do-o-o?*
*It's more that I can bear,*
*Oh, sis, I searched for you everywhere!*
*Now, please tell me where to go, what to do*
*I can't go anywhere without you-u!*

*Mai, now I am alone*
*I just can't find you*
*not even one single bone*

*I couldn't find one single clue.*
*With being sad, I just can't stop*
*because you all are gone now*
*feel like I will fall right from the top*
*and I won't fall on soft snow!*

*Oh Mai, I have searched for you,*
*a whole year without any clue*
*someone tell me... what should I do-o-o?*
*It's more that I can bear,*
*Oh, sis, I searched for you everywhere!*
*Now, please tell me where to go, what to do*
*I can't go anywhere without you-u!*

As Achak stopped he tried to transform back to a human boy, but it did not work. So Achak lied down and fell asleep.

When Achak woke he did not notice the stinging pain in his back. He had to go, now was dawn which was the perfect time. He knew as a wolf he would be much faster at the other mountain. So, he began to walk, in his big werewolf form he had better chances of hunting. He went to look for prey but traveled at the same time to the                    light                    mountains. Achak was hungry, but he did not find any prey. I bet the humans already killed the whole prey, he thought sadly. No wonder he did not hear anything of his cousins, aunts, uncles, and friends of the light pack since he was nine, the humans have killed the whole prey! And… maybe even his cousins Bodaway, Chaska, Chatan, Chitto, Dyami, Elsu, Abey, Atsila and Devaki. His aunts Dena, Fala, Isi and Kish. His uncles Lakota, Lanato, Migisi, Nahele and Rowtag. His three friends Sucki, Wattan and Yansa. He would feel terrible if that were so, but deep inside him there were two voices fighting. *"You know they're all dead so why the hopes? Your whole family is dead, even your friends! You are the last werewolf!"* *"Now that's not true there is still a werewolf, you know him. The chief of the thunder pack; Annawan."* *"Oh, bloody full moon, if Annawan is dead, you'll have no chance!"*

"Enough!" Achak yelled, he did not care that it came as a howl out of his mouth. The positive voice in him was right, Annawan! He was the chief of the thunder pack. Achak and Annawan first met when Annawan was about 15 years old and Achak eight or… was he nine? Never mind, he and Annawan understood each other incredibly good. He was one of the strongest Werewolves Achak ever saw. But there was more about Annawan, something Achak could not say, Annawan was tall with black hair and brown eyes. Just like Achak, but as a werewolf, Annawan has got light-brown fur, which was exceedingly rare. A werewolf with black hair as a human and with bright fur as a werewolf were exceedingly rare! That was one of the things which fascinated Achak about

Annawan, even the fact that both their names began with an "A". It was pretty funny, the most typical werewolf names started with an "A", and still only a few werewolves' names started with an "A".

Achak shook his head to clear his mind. Maybe the more negative voice was right too… No, he had to find Annawan and give up the search for Mai.

Time passed, Achak did not have a lot of stuff with him. If it were so he would have needed a Capricorn or chamois or a pony, a goat or even a reindeer. In the most, if not all, werewolf-clans and -packs they used such animals to help them carry a lot of things. Mostly the Clans that were nomads used them. Achak knew that also the dark-mountain-pack used such animals that were good at climbing.
In the day Achak slept and in the night he traveled. In the night when he traveled, he always looked for food. In his pack he, his brothers, his sister, his cousins, and his friends often had to practice their survival techniques as humans. That was extremely important, just like hunting with bow and arrow or controlling their temper or for Achak, controlling his transformations. Still, he spent lots of time as a wolf, but for the survival practice he always was in human form. Or also just to climb the mountains. And now, he was glad he was in that survival practice, practicing his climbing. Because now, his instincts told him what to do, what the best way was to build his

shelter or what berries he could eat. So, at dawn he searched for berries he could eat without using much energy. He found some raspberries, blackberries, and blueberries he could eat. He even saw a hare, that was a welcome snack, assuming he would hit the hare. He took one of his arrows, drew his bow, released and... missed. Again. Oh, by the seven mountain pikes! *Why cannot I just hit once*, he asked himself. Maybe it was because of his bow or his arrows or even both? Achak searched for an elm to build a new bow. First, he had to cut the tree to a good size, about chest high, then he took an ax to chop the wood into the right form. That took long, and to Achak it seemed like ages. And when he finally finished with chopping, he had to make a score for the tendon. And when Achak finished with that as well, he made a fire. Over the fire he held a lump of resin and wax until it was smooth enough to rub it into the wood, so the wood would not get wet when it rains. To protect the wood, he had to massage the mixture of wax and resin into the wood. Now he only had to make a tendon. For that he took four fibers of hemp on one end he had to knot the for fibers, and then he drilled them to a tendon. He also rubbed the tendon with the wax-resin mixture. After that he attached the tendon to the bow ends. Now he had to make the arrows. First, he needed some hazelnut wood and a fire. He searched for straight sticks, because they would fly better, at least he hopped so. When Achak had four straight sticks he searched for birch trees, to get some birch pitch, so he could stick three feathers on to the back of the arrow. When he had the birch pitch, he first chopped a bit of the arrow-stick so that the wood was as long as his arm. Then he made a score for the string of the bow, he also polished the score with horsetail. Now he spread the birch pitch over the arrow and attached the feathers and sharpened the arrowhead. After the arrows dried, he prepared to hunt. At sundown Achak went to a waterhole and waited. And waited. Then, he finally saw a pheasant that began to drink. Achak drew the bow. Released. And… hit! "Yeah! I… I hit", he went to the dying animal and looked it in the eye. "Thanks, my friend. I am sorry that I killed you, but I need your meat to survive." Achak ate the bird and continued his journey.

After 14 Sunsets, in the night at moonrise, Achak crossed the way of a lynx. The lynx stared at the werewolf, Achak growled. The lynx suddenly spoke "Hey who are you? Are you a werewolf?" Achak did not really know what he did as he nodded. He was too surprised. The lynx said excitedly, "Really, cool. Wait right here! Wait here! I've got to tell this to Annawan!"

# Chapter 3

Annawan? The lynx was already gone. But did Achak hear right, did the lynx really say Annawan? Yes! Yes, he did! Before Achak could think more he saw a great werewolf with light-brown fur with orange-red eyes. The wolf walked straight to Achak behind him, the lynx. As the werewolf saw Achak they both ran up to each other both thinking they were the last of their kind, but no! They both found another one. Finally, the bright werewolf spoke, "Achak? Is that you?" Achak saw the lynx, he looked a bit confused. That must be because the two wolves were talking in their own language. "Yes! And... Annawan?" The other werewolf began to wag his tail. "Yes! Oh finally! Why are you here? What happened? Where are the others?" Annawan was asking quite fast, but Achak understood him. Annawan and Achak have not seen each other for about three years!

"I am here because I was searching for you... And... what happened..." Annawan understood, he liked the dark mountain pack, mostly Achak, Mai, Tokala, Hakan, Tala and Tocho. Annawan threw his head back and let out a painful howl. Achak joined and they both howled. And then suddenly they noticed that the lynx was still here!

Oh, mighty snowstorm, did the lynx understand why they were howling? No, he did not speak the werewolf language, thank Acaraho! "Adahy, you go back and tell Kai Redfur that Achak, a werewolf, will come soon. Okay?" The lynx nodded and ran away. Annawan turned his head to Achak and they both spoke again.

"Annawan? Where did the lynx just go?"

"Adahy? He went back to the Nahuelschool. There I live in the moment. It's the only place where humans don't hunt for me. You know, I accidentally transformed in front of a human, they were all so frightened at my sight. They began to haunt me, so I had to hide, but unfortunately a famous werewolf-hunter named Julia La Lune found me. And... oh dear, I guess you know what happened right?" Achak nodded, Annawan too? Phou, so he was not the only one who made a mistake. While they were walking to the school deep in the forest, they were talking. Achak told Annawan what had happened a year ago, Annawan told him about the school. It was a school for three types, Shapeshifters, Witches and Wizards and Werewolves, though, Annawan was the only one. He somehow knew he would be the only werewolf but in case the school had some books for werewolves.

They arrived. Achak stared at the big building, while Annawan transformed into a human. Achak looked at him, as a human Annawan was tall with short black hair and brown eyes. Achak tried to transform as well but he felt the stinging pain in his back. He yelled. Annawan looked at him. "Everything okay?" He stepped closer to Achak and looked at his back. "Uh that looks bad. A shot I suppose?" The werewolf nodded. Annawan nodded and said: "Okay…hmm… Steffi, Steve come quick! Achak has got a gaze shot!"

Two squirrels came out of the door at the sight of the great, black werewolf they stopped and transformed into humans, a woman, and a man. They both had nut-brown hair and eyes and came to him. They seemed to be the healers. The woman, Steffi, went and came packed with some bandages. As they were finished Achak tried again to transform, it worked, though, he yelled loudly while transforming back to a human boy. Annawan stepped to him and laid a hand on Achaks shoulder. Steve and Steffi went back inside while Annawan showed Achak where he could sleep. Achak liked the idea to stay with Annawan, so he followed Annawan into the building.

"If you want to stay, you'll need your own room. There are still a few left so… you can choose one, they are all different you know? You can make yourself at home though I know it'll never be like the mountains…" Annawan sounded sad but as he continued, he sounded more confident. "Well, I will show you around. If you want to stay, you'll have to take part in class. But you can tell me tomorrow, so… yea." Annawan left and Achak was searching for one of the rooms. He checked every room, the last one was the best, he thought. Through the window he could see the moon, the forest, the mountains and the sunset. There was one bed, a desk, a closet and a bookshelf. Suddenly it knocked at the door, Achak looked to the door and saw three boys standing there. One of them – the one with brown hair and orange-brown eyes – stepped forward

"Hi, I'm Adahy and this is Dexter," he pointed at the boy with fire red hair and sand- brown eyes, "and Adam" he pointed towards the boy with brown hair with some grey and blue eyes. "we're shapeshifters. You're the black werewolf, right?"

"Aha… Hi I am Achak, yes I am a black werewolf. Are you the lynx who brought Annawan to me? And what forms do you guys take?"

"Yes, I am that lynx," Adahy responded. "Annawan was quite wild on finding another werewolf. And by the way Dex takes the form of a…"

"… a red fox." Dexter replied.

"And I'm a wolf. A grey wolf to be to be exact. So, do you need anything?" Adam asked. Achak looked around, well the ceiling needed some black of the night and the shine of the white stars, the walls maybe some grey or green and the bed… well he could figure that out later. So, he just shook his head. The three boys nodded and left the room.

Achak looked closer at the bookshelf. There were already books in dear! Achak always was a curious werewolf, and so he went to the books. Λεσ θατρε τυπεσ δε λουπσ-γαρουσ, it said, in the old language of the werewolves and even the old writing. Luckily Achak knew the old werewolf-writing. So, he translated it. Les quatre types de loups-garous, it said. But it was written very complicatedly, so that Achak needed a while to understand, The four types of werewolves. If Achak did not know better, he would say that was what the humans called, French. Achak was so curious, he looked inside. It was sort of a diary. Achak looked if it was signed, and... yes! It was! And not only that, but it was also signed by one of the werewolves who were especially important for the werewolf history! Angeni! The god of the Spirit! Of freedom, of the wild! And, Achaks great-great-great-great grandmother! Wow! Achak wanted to show Annawan, after all he was a werewolf to!

"You are kidding me, right? The diary of Angeni! Wow!" Annawan was excited. Achak opened the book on the first page and read loudly:

*A terrible day for all the wildmoon werewolves! As we all know, there are four types of werewolves. By the way, the title is just a disguise, so not everybody will read it. The lokoti werewolf, the north American werewolf, the Asian werewolf, and the European werewolf. But Story tells of a fifth werewolf type named the wildmoon werewolf. In this time there are only two known wildmoon werewolves, Jacy and Shiriki, the twins. We're not really sure if they are wildmoon werewolves but after all the tales and stories about wildmoon werewolves they must've been. They could transform whenever they wanted and looked like normal gray wolves, but they're eyes glowed green and ice blue. So, we can guess they are wildmoons. But a moon ago something terrible happened! Jacy and Shiriki were 21, and by the last full moon Jacy lost control and was shot by the werewolf-hunter Stefan La Lune! By the loss of his brother Shiriki went mad, stole the old scroll of the fire-twins Atsila and Rowtag! Now no one knows where he is. But we all know that the scroll beholds the most important legend - or prophesy? – about the end of the werewolves and that two wildmoon werewolves will put an end to the La Lunes.*

### *Angeni the Free one*

"Wow! The end of the werewolves? That's now! Bloody Thunderstorm", Annawan said. Achak was confused. Two wildmoon werewolves? A mixture out of all four werewolf types? Eyes glowing, transforming whenever they wanted? But that sounded like him and Annawan. Now! Yes!... That couldn't be. Yes, the end of their kind is near... rubbish it is here!

"Come on Achak! Let's read the next side, maybe there is more about that!

"Yes! Good idea Annawan!" He read loudly:

*The La Lunes have been successful! They shot my little brother Shiriki too! Eight moons ago Stefan La Lune shot my little brother Jacy and now Shiriki too! I wish I could transform into a tree and sleep forever! I wish I could sink into the ground. Now the Thunder clan werewolves are without a chief, too! And the worst thing, I must lead the dark mountain pack and my biggest brother Annawan must now lead the Thunder clan and his oldest son who is named Keme will be the next chief.*

"Oh Acaraho! That's terrible! The La Lunes did the same thing to Angeni like they did to us! Just thousands of moons ago!" Achak yelled. He felt compassion, affection and felt sorry for his great-great-great-great grandmother. She must've known exactly how he and Annawan feel right now.

"The La Lunes have always hunted our kind... but now... Annawan I think they finally reached their goal. I mean my family, my friends, just like yours... we are the last werewolves." "I know... Is there a next page?"

"Uhm..." Achak turned over several pages till... "Yes! But... it's another handwriting."

*Oh Acaraho, Heinmot! Why!? Why did you have to take Angeni too? The bravest werewolf of our time! She saved my little daughter Iye. She was so happy and optimistic, even after her brothers got shot. And now she's gone too! My best friend. Angeni we will never forget you!*

*Catori the friendly*

"Gasps. That's horrible! Annawan, why do the humans do such things?" In Annawans face, the sorrow was visible.

30

"Annawan?" Achak looked at his older friend. Annawan looked back and said, with a low voice which sounded not more than a whisper.

"Catori and Iye where my… my… Catori was my great-great-great-great-grandmother and Iye my great-great-great-grandmother. You know that we mostly get to know our great-great-great-grandparents and when we're lucky even our great-great-great-great-grandparents, right?" Achak nodded and Annawan said: "Well I got to know Iye and she told me that her mother told her of the little brothers of her best friend. And how Shiriki suffered from the loss of his twin brother. How he stole the ancient scroll of the fire twins Atsila and Rowtag. And how he got shot by Stefan La Lune." Achak looked Annawan in the eyes, he had light tears in his brown eyes. Annawan shook his head and Achak knew that his friend had to be alone for a bit. "I'll see you later, then." Without another word Achak left the room leaving a distressed Annawan behind.

As the sun was setting, Achak sat outside of the building, as he saw a woman with long curly blond hair and cold blue eyes. The typical signs of a La Lune!

# Chapter 4

Oh-oh! Achak stood up and ran back to Annawan, though he nearly fell after standing up, he was so fast.

"Annawan! Lei è qui, Julia La Lune! She's here!" Annawan stormed out of the room where the two of them read the diary of Angeni. Without noticing it they both fell back to the old werewolf-language, which was a mix of Latin, bit French, Italian and a Language, humans can't understand. "Bene, debemus manere tranquillitas! Altrimenti uta leratuke!"

"Si! Calme, calme!" They were saying something like; "She's here Julia La Lune!" "Ok, we've got to stay calm or she'll get suspicious"

"Yes, calm, calm!"

The two werewolves did not notice that the three shapeshifters Adahy, Adam and Dexter were standing right behind them and heard everything. Dexter asked: "Ahm... What were you saying?" A man with brown hair and blue eyes came to them and said to Annawan: "A woman just a..."

"I know Kai, Achak already told me!" Annawans voice was full of panic and fear, also Achak felt the fear in his soul but also the burning anger. It was that woman's fault his family was dead! He got angry and began to transform, but not only he was transforming, also on Annawans arms brown fur was beginning to spread.

"Annawan, Achak if you two transform in front of Julia La Lune you'll get a free ticket straight to hell, or... whatever you werewolves say!", Kai yelled. But naturally it didn't stop, Achak felt long fangs growing and saw how Annawan became pointy brown ears. He heard how Kai spoke some bad curses before speaking.

"Ok, Adahy, Adam you two got to distract La Lune. Dex, you got to tell the other teachers and students, tell Chatan and Jack that I need some help with the two wolves." The three nodded and spread out. Meanwhile Achak felt slowly long sharp claws growing, and how he became a tail and then... Snapp... He was sitting there as a large wolf, next to him sat a wolf with brown fur and orange-red eyes. Kai gasped in relief as other men came "Holy sky!" The man with grey hair and yellow eyes said as he looked at the wolves. "Jack, you gotta help me." The other man nodded, and together they brought the two wolves to a safe place to transform back, while Kai should go and speak with Julia La Lune.

"I don't wanna stay here while Julia La Lune is out there!" Annawan said furious. "She killed my whole pack! My father, my little sisters and my younger brother Koko!" As a wolf Annawan let out a howl full of sadness and frustration. Jack frightened but looked strictly at Annawan blaming him for his loud cry. "Annawan look I know you're headmaster but you can't just cry like that, what if Julia heard you?" Annawan did not answer. Achak knew how he felt, but suddenly he smelled something... familiar. He could smell gunpowder and then he heard something but could not identify it.

"Where are the werewolves?", a female voice said. "I know there are the last werewolves. They are here!"

"I'm sorry but if there were werewolves at the school our headmaster Annawan would know..." That was Kai talking to Julia La Lune!

"Annawan? That's a typical werewolf name! Bring me to him, now!" Jack and Chatan forced Annawan and Achak into a little room to transform.

"Oh, bloody thunderstorm! Julia La Lune's here and we can't do anything about it!" Annawan cried as he was back in human form. Achak nodded. "Listen, we have to go outside without hurting her, or otherwise... she'll know! We've got to stay calm."

"You're right my friend", Annawan answered. "Come on!"

Together they left the room and searched for Julia La Lune and Kai. They found them outside.

"... wan is a typical werewolf-name, it means chief. You've got a new student, named Achak? Well, that's a werewolf name too. It means Spirit. But I'm sure you know that, right?" She didn't let Kai answer but just wanted to start talking again as Annawan and Achak came.

"Is there a problem?", Annawan asked calmly. Of his nervousness from before there was no remainder. He spoke calmly as he said to Julia La Lune: "I'm sorry that I just arrived to speak with you Miss La Lune, but I had a very important call from my Dad. You know my Mother's extremely ill and she wanted to talk with me." Annawan invented. "And then, I'm sure you know how that is, she just couldn't stop talking, till I said that we've got visitors at the school."

"Aha," Julia La Lune said now softly. "Then I'm sorry for my overreaction. But I'm sure you know; I'm looking for two werewolves. One of them was only sited as a wolf with light-brown fur and the other one is a boy which looks just like him," she said pointing at Achak. "But of course, why should you let a werewolf in the school? Well then, I'm sorry. Bye!" Suddenly she was in a rush. And disappeared in the forest.

Three days have passed since the werewolf hunter Julia La Lune was at the school to find the last werewolves. Annawan decided that they both need "normal" clothes and today they will go both together to the nearby village to buy some clothes. Some of the teachers gave them money. The werewolves called the coins "little full moons" because they were shining and round like a full moon. Annawan also called them "Silver pool" and the cash – even though Annawan was nearly a year or even two by the humans, the teachers explained to them –

they called it "small grass clearing". Annawan became about 200 bees (Money in general also by the humans) and Achak 240 bees. Achak became a bit more because Annawan already had 40 bees on his own.

"You both got to be really careful. Annawan I know you're the headmaster but in this case it's better if I take over," Kai added as Annawan wanted to say something. "Even though you're already one and a half years here at this school you still don't really fit in. You just need to learn more after all you're just 18 you can actually speak of luck that no one found out yet!" Annawan did not say anything, he just nodded his head with an amused little smile. It did not seem to bother Annawan what Kai said. Kai seemed to be a bit confused because of that.

"I bet your parents had a rough time with you and Mai. My father never said if we should or should not do something, except that we never may go near the human village. So, if I wanted to go and explore the forest my father let me. If I wanted to see a bear right after the leaf empty session, my father would let me."

"You called it leaves empty? We always had a few names to call it; Puma time or snowfall."

"Yeah, humans call the time winter – that is snowfall – spring is flower return, then there is summer in the thunder Clan we call it the thunder time and autumn, by us leaf fall. Crazy ideas, right?" Achak nodded his head and they walked further. Achak could see the village. He and Annawan both took a deep breath, and then they entered the village.

"Okay little one, in… one hour and 30 minutes will meet here. Alright?"

"Jap see yah!" They split up and went in different directions, Annawan went to a shop with shoes and Achak went to a clothes shop.

When he entered the shop, Achak rather turned and ran out. In the shop there were not only clothes but also some stuffed animals. But before Achak could turn around a woman came to him and asked: "Excuse me! Can I help you?" Achak startled and looked at the woman. She had blond hair and green-brown eyes and she smiled friendly.

"Ahm… yeah. I need some clothes for… winter and summer?" Achak was a bit unsure but the woman laughed and said: "I guess you never were shopping alone right?" Achak nodded. "Well follow me, I think we got some shirts, and shorts for now. After all it still takes six months till it'll get freezing cold." Achak followed the woman until she stopped. "Here you can choose and then try them on over there", she pointed to some cabins. "And then you can pay." The woman went again and Achak looked by himself for clothes. He found a beige short, a black short and a blue short. And about three black T-Shirts, a blue one, four yellow-red Shirts, two green and five brown T-Shirts. After he tried them all, he went to pay. One T-Shirt only cost five bees. "That will be 105 bees." Holy grasslands that's plenty! Achak thought. He paid and went with the clothes in a bag to another shop. Not a shoe shop, but a shop with necklaces. He never liked the thought of leather on his feet. But he always liked necklaces. After all he did once have a necklace with a claw of a puma which was sticking in a tree. But he lost it on the night of the big fight. On the night of the end of the dark mountain pack.

He shook his head; he didn't want to think about that. Not now. Now he wanted to see if there was a necklace which would suit him. Achak liked that shop a bit better, because there was no animal fur at the walls or stuffed animals. There were just a lot of necklaces. Achak looked for a while until he found a cool necklace. A necklace with a silver full moon as a pendant. Achak wanted to touch it but then he remembered that he could not touch silver. No matter if I just try, he said to himself. Slowly he touched the necklace but didn't feel a burning like he once did as he touched silver in a village. Gladness overcame him and he took that necklace, paid 50 bees and then he went back to the spot Annawan and he agreed to meet again. He didn't have to wait long, Annawan came in quite a hurry. "Come Achak, quick we got to go!" Achak followed Annawan back to the forest. "Annawan, what's the matter?" Achak asked. When they were back in the forest Annawan stopped, looked at Achak and said quietly: "It's La Lune. She made a video and a photo of us. As werewolves and humans! It came in the news. Achak we must get back to the school immediately!"

Achak did not deny what he said. Then, after a few moments, Achak and Annawan walked through the forest to the village.

In the forest Achak felt nearly at home, there were no stones big enough to hide or to climb on them. In this forest the ground was almost straight, not that steep like the forest ground in his old home, where forest and mountains were one. Something, which was also different was that this forest did not seem to have a little creek with clear mountain water. And in this forest, there were both evergreens and deciduous trees, while in his old forest there were mostly evergreens and extremely little deciduous trees.

"This forest is so different from the forest I grew up in. I always thought there must be at least a little creek or some rocks." Achak said suddenly.

"I know this must be different, but I grew up in a similar forest near the prairie. It was wonderful, and in the night... you had a clear sight in the sky, at the moon and the stars." Annawan was explaining to Achak how his younger siblings always made Annawan take them out and how he nearly got himself killed when he got in the way of a bison stampede. And Achak told how he and his sister nearly fell off the devil cliff and climbed the huge ravine where Mai broke a leg and Achak a couple of rips.

When they were in the school Kai, Jack, Adahy, Adam and Dex came to them with a newspaper in their hands. "You're in the news", Jack said. "On the front page! Here read from Julia La Lune."

Achak couldn't read but he knew what was on the frontpage, because Kai held the paper that Achak could look at and because Kai read loudly. **"Werewolves in a school!"**

# Chapter 5

"The famous werewolf hunter Julia La Lune found the "Last Werewolves" Like she says. Julia La Lune claims that the last werewolves are the rare werewolf species which are called wild- moon werewolves. They seem to be extremely wild and dangerous. The names of the werewolves are Achak and Annawan. Keep your eyes open!" Kai read loudly and then he showed a picture of them, Achak as a boy with chin long, black curled hair and brown eyes, and as a great black wolf. And Annawan was a man with shorter black hair and wood brown eyes, and a huge brown wolf with yellow glowing eyes. "Mighty Snowstorm," Achak said, while Annawan rather looked upset. And then Kai said: "Annawan, Achak, you two can't go out anymore. Or you'll get caught!" Achak and Annawan contradicted.

"What? No!"

"That's not fair!"

"Yeah, we need to get out!"

"Annawan's right..."

But Kai just said: "You two need to get better control! Annawan you're just 18 going on 19. You can't risk getting killed! And you Achak are... 12, right? Do you really want to risk your life just because you want to go outside?" Kai did not wait for an answer, instead he and Jack forced the two werewolves inside the school. They brought them to Achaks room so they could calm down. "So, you two will stay here until dinner okay?" And with those words, Kai and Jack shut the door.

"Wow I'd newer, thought that they'd actually do that." Annawan said, impressed. "What?" "That they'll lock me up if I ever lose control. But, we're right, that we have to stay inside is just not fair!"

"Yeah, but in one direction there right. We shouldn't risk our life because of La Lune. We got to – oh Acaraho I can't believe I'm saying this – but we got to be patient." Annawan smirked and then he said: "Maybe we should try our new clothes."

Achaks face lit up and he and Annawan tried on their new clothes. It took a while until Achak chose the beige shorts, the brown T-Shirt, and the full moon necklace. Then he went to a merrow and looked at himself. Achak looked at a young boy with curly black hair, the sun shined from the side of his eyes, so they glowed amber brown. He looked at his clothes, they suit him. Then Achak heard steps and turned around. Annawan stood behind him, with blue shorts, a grey colored T-Shirt, and a necklace with a silver paw as pendant. Shoes he did not wear, but a bracelet out of black hair, as pendant, a silver cloud with a lightning pendant.

"You look good Achak." Annawan said with a grin. "So do you, thundercloud." Achak looked a second time in the merrow and thought that the clothes looked good but also a little ridiculous. The two waited till Kai would let the two out so they could eat something and to pass the time they talked.

"Ok Achak I want to know where you lived and how it was there."

"By the seven mountain pikes, that's easy. I grew up in the dark mountains, do you know where that is?" Annawan nodded. "Good, the dark mountains, the black forest – it wasn't really black – and the grasslands all around was once my territory. In the dark mountains there were loads of rocks, cliffs, caves, evergreens, little streams and the higher you get the more snow there was. I loved the forest in the mountains, like I said there were rocks and trees and caves, it never was near boring. I lived mostly as a wolf, my parents did not know why I could transform also by daylight when I want but… yeah, they still taught me a lot. When I slowly began to control my transformations, I spent more time as a human. Mai and I explored new hidings and began to hunt. I must admit, I was… no I am no good hunter, but to test myself I did it, even though I never caught something in human form, I mean only two legs and ridiculous little teeth! But never mind, I told you that there were lots of cliffs. I loved to climb, not only because my whole pack was not good at climbing, but also because I was really good. I climbed in the forest on trees, on the bigger and higher rocks and sometimes when I wanted to be alone, I tried to climb up to the peaks, sometimes I was successful. When I did, I mostly slept one or two nights somewhere on that mountain I climbed on. And... no, now it's your turn."

"Ok where should I start..." Annawan asked, more to himself than to Achak, and yet he answered:

"How about where you grew up?"

"Good idea," Annawan responded. "Ok I grew up in the thunder forest you know where...?"

"Yes."

"Okay, by the Thunder clan we all live in little lairs and with seven we search for an own sleeping place. About half of the forest together with a lake and plenty of grasslands was the territory of my pack. With seven I had to leave the lair of my mother and my younger siblings. So, I looked for my lair, you know, my territory was huge, it took a whole day until I found a lair. It was a hole under a tree, I tried to get in there and that was the first time I transformed into a normal Wolf... pup. Well, I fit in the hole, but it was a bit small, I had to dig the rest until it was big enough for me. When I was ten, I decided to try three whole days as Wolf, without my family noticing. That was the hardest part, but I managed to tell them I was exploring the territory and testing myself. I was lucky that they believed me. But I had trouble finding the correct plants to eat, after all you can not only eat meat, right? What did you eat Achak?"

"Well in the mountains there are not a lot of plants, we actually eat everything we could." Achak smiled. Most werewolf packs have their own eating habits. Plants, meat, fish, plants and fish, plants, and meat... those things. But the werewolves of the dark mountains had to eat other things than just meat. They did not always have enough meat for the whole pack because they did it as humans. The only time they had enough meat was during the full moon. But as humans they hunted the animals that lived in the mountains and the forest like, marmots, snowshoe hares, alpine chough, fallow deer, squirrels, rabbits, hares, red deer or if they were lucky even an elk. But they did not only hunt, if they did so the animals would be extinct around the mountains. So, to avoid that, they also eat plants, worms, snails or other insects or spiders, even though they are not full afterwards. "We ate everything that was edible, except the eagles, falcons and other predators. But what we also did was fishing. That was what we ate at leaf fall nearly all the time. There were a lot of fish in the loads of rivers and streams..."

"Annawan? Achak? Did you calm down a bit", Kai's voice asked suddenly. "Yeah, I think so, except you give us something to eat." Annawan responded.

Kai grinned and said then: "Yes, the wolf pack and Adahy went extra hunting for Annawan because he only eats meat. Except maybe if you threaten him. But without that... forget it." Annawan smiled, said thank you to Kai and then he and Achak went to the dining hall. Achak could hear Annawan and Kai talking about something, but he could not hear what they were talking about.

When they arrived in the great hall Achak looked around. There are a lot of small and bigger tables, a lot of children and teachers and plenty of food. "Why is this such a big pack? I mean... This is my... second week here, actually funny that I never eat in this hall." Achak said to himself. When he saw Adahy, Adam and Dex he hesitated. Should he go to them? Before he could think longer Adahy looked at him and made a sign which meant that Achak should come to them. So Achak sat to them and asked immediately: "So, what did you hunt?"

"Well, we just hunted a boar for Annawan, it is big enough for you both. But, well I thought that wolves of the dark mountains eat everything, right? I once read something about that." Adahy added when he saw that Achak wanted to ask why he knew that. They began to eat until Annawan began to speak.

"Listen everybody," he shouted, and every single person stopped talking and listened. "You all know that the werewolf hunter Julia La Lune was here because she searched for Achak and me. Now to those who don't know who Achak is, he's the last werewolf next to me and a descendant of the dark mountain pack. But that's another subject, because the reason that I am speaking is that the teachers and I decided that I'm too young to run the school! I am just 18 and now that we have two werewolves, the teachers and I decided that Achak and I will take part in class. My successor will be Chatan, the teacher for survival and fight." Chatan stepped to

Annawan and began to speak: "Yes, Annawan that is true, so like Annawan said, he and Achak will be part of your class by tomorrow. So now, enjoy your meal."

Annawan came to them – Achak, Adahy, Adam and Dex – after most of the students began to eat. "So, well that is a bit of a relief. Now I am not responsible for what is going on here." Annawan sat with his younger friend and they began to eat.

In the night Achak could not sleep. He was thinking and thinking and thinking of Julia La Lune and of the wildmoon werewolf, why were they so rare? Why did they go extinct? How old is the wildmoon werewolf already known? And why, by the mighty snowstorm why are the La Lunes so wild on hunting werewolves to their end? Achak just wanted to know the answers. Knowing that he would not sleep even if he tried, he left his room and walked in the corridors to get his mind off things. Achak came to a big window where he could see the moon. It was not full moon yet, but close. The moon's light shined bright and Achak saw everything around, suddenly he noticed a second person coming, just before he could vanish in the shadows the person stepped in the moonlight. It was Annawan. His black was wet, and his eyes glowed in pain. Achak was frightened, Annawan was much happier at dinner.

"Annawan", he asked. "What happened?"

"Nothing happened, Achak. I... just had a bad dream. Nothing serious."

"Nothing serious? I do not believe that. Look at you."

"I'm fine Achak!", Annawan responded angry. "I just had a bad dream!"

"That's what you say! Annawan, when I was walking from the dark mountains to find you, I often had bad dreams. I know when someone had a bad dream. And you look just like that! You've got wet hair, and I don't think that you went for a swim." Annawan opened his mouth to defend himself but Achak was already explaining. "And your eyes are glowing, not only in pain, but also red. Those are signs for a nightmare!"

"... alright. Yes! I had a bad nightmare! I dreamed about the day my clan was destroyed!" Annawans voice suddenly sounded like the one of a cub. And Achak knew why his eyes were glowing because he cried just a bit earlier. "It reminded me of everything, my siblings getting killed, my cousins, friends, my whole clan!" A wave of bitterness broke over him, in the speed of the wind of the storms in the mountains, and in the speed the weather could change and surprise you if you didn't grow up there. The anger towards Julia La Lune burned in him and nearly exploded when Achak thought of his last day with his pack.

"Julia killed my father personally. She killed most of my mates and brothers. Nearly she even killed me, if... if my father didn't pull me away, I could have been killed too."

Achak knew how Annawan must feel. He remembered that he sang to express his feelings. "Hey, ahm, Annawan. Maybe we could sing together, you know, I did that after my pack was slaughtered." Annawans eyes lightened up. It was clear that he waited just until someone would come who would sing. Of course, without saying "no". They both sat in werewolf form in front of the window. And they began to sing, letting all their emotions flow out.

*Here we are, trapped, because of Julia La Lune,*
*To her weapons, her cruelty we are not immune.*
*We both lost our families, friends, and all other mates,*
*does it have to be that way, was that really all their*
*fates?*
*Life isn't fair, but why did a lot of life end this way?*
*Why can't so many werewolves experience the next*
*day?*
*It's just not fair! We once said we'd protect the pack,*
*but now, we only see black.*
*Where once a bunch of colors were,*
*there's now, a dead atmosphere.*
*We lived our life, but how could we all know,*
*that, the humans will force us all to go!?*
*But that's just the typical human way,*
*to destroy and turn everything into an unfair play!*
*We werewolves just do what we gotta do,*

*and humans destroy everything like the clans of me and you!*

They changed with singing, Achak, Annawan, Achak and then Annawan again. Achak began with the first rhyme, and Annawan sang the second one, and so they always changed with who is singing. But now they both had to stop. Because Annawan knew that they would be tired tomorrow in class if they do not sleep. But neither Achak nor Annawan wanted to sleep in their own rooms.
"We'll just sleep together as wolves. Maybe here in the moonlight" Annawan suggested. Achak nodded his mighty wolf head. He found it quite cool that he and Annawan could speak, not only as humans but also as wolves. And not only to each other, but also with other animals. That was cool, especially when you are trapped or something like that, the ability of the normal animal language is quite a profit.
Now Achak and Annawan just rested as wolves in the shining moonlight, cuddled next to each other.

In the morning, Achak and Annawan woke up because of lots of voices, of teachers and students.
"How did they do that?"
"I don't know, it isn't a full moon yet."
"But how did they transform to werewolves even though the full moon isn't here?"
"Maybe they're wildmoon werewolves?"

"I once heard something like that, but it's said that they are aggressive, but actually Annawan isn't so aggressive." Achak opened his eyes and saw a bunch of students who all were staring at Achak and Annawan, in their wolf forms! Also, Annawan must have noticed because suddenly his brown wolf head was not next to Achak. Instead Annawan looked at the people with a sort of calmness in his eyes. Then, a grey-brown wolf stepped forward, and spoke shy:

"… I don't know if you understand me but…" That was Adam. Annawan just answered with a "Yes we can understand you" and then he let Adam speak again.

"Oh… great! So, we all wanna know, how did you transform into normal werewolves, without the full moon?"

Achak and Annawan looked at each other, Annawan nodded his fury head, Achak nodded towards Adam. But did not transform back into a human. He sat on his hindlegs and looked at Adam.

"Well, it could be", Achak began a bit shy. "Annawan and I. We are wildmoon werewolves." Achak ended as fast as he could, but still so that Adam could understand him. Adam looked at the two werewolves, unbelief in his eyes. But then he nodded, transformed into the human boy with brown hair, some grey in them and blue eyes he was. Adam explained to the others what he heard. The teachers said nothing, while the students began to whisper and look at the two werewolves which felt a bit uncomfortable. Then out of nowhere, Kai stood there in front of the others and spoke:

"Look guys. We all must stay calm. Yes, wildmoons are not famous for their soft manner, but we all know that there are special cases which do not fit with the idea of that thing. Like the werewolves." The teachers nodded and the students were quiet. What are they going to say? Achak asked himself. And to his surprise the students all just walked to their classrooms. Annawan looked thankfully at Kai, who did not hesitate to ask:

"How do you know that you are wildmoons?"

"Well actually... it's simple," Annawan explained. "Wildmoons can transform even by daylight, just like us, and there are other things which I do not want to explain."

Kai looked at the two werewolves – which already transformed back – and then he nodded. "Go to your classes."

Without another word Achak and Annawan went straight to one of the dozens of classrooms and entered.

"Which subject do we have now?", Achak whispered to Annawan because he did not want to draw attention to him and Annawan.

"... Oh no! Human study with Alaika!" Annawan gasped. Achak looked rather spiteful. Why on earth did they have to study humans? Achak knew already enough, their spiteful, bad, nasty creatures which have no respect for nature and animals!

"Why that?"

"Well, I guess it's sort of a warning to us, or… mostly at shapeshifters and the witches and wizards. After all, werewolves do not live among humans. We live outside, in nature. From the deepest forests over the widest grassland, the farthest lakes to the highest mountains. That is our habitat. But thanks to the humans," Annawans voice grew angry and louder. "We both have to stay here, while there could still be some werewolves out there without their packs. Other clans and packs get slaughtered and our whole kind goes extinct!"

Annawan shouted the last few words so loudly, that a few students looked at them. Achak did not care what others think of him, he never did. And right now, he just had to agree with the other wildmoon werewolf. Every time when packs and clans got hunted down, there was always at least someone who survived the fight against the humans. But those were most of the time cubs, around five to ten which survived the fight, but then got killed by hunters, traps or just because they do not know how to survive alone.

Then, without that Achak noticed a woman entered the room. Achak still was busy with cursing the humans for their existence. But he snapped out of his thoughts, as Annawan gave him a nudge in the ribs. First Achak looked angry at Annawan for interrupting his thoughts, until he noticed that woman entered the room. She was big with long blond hair and blue eyes.

"Well then, if also the young werewolves would pay attention we could start with class." Oh, grate, Achak thought. My first day and she already hates me.

"Don't worry," Annawan whispered to Achak. "She doesn't like me either. I suppose she is afraid of werewolves or just dislikes them. Even when I was the headmaster, she didn't like me."

"MHM... I would like to begin with class, without interruptions!"

# Chapter 6

"Oh finally! I thought human study would never end!" Achak gasped when he and Annawan could finally get out of that classroom. "What's next?"

"Survival and fight, short saf, with Chatan!" Annawan sounded much happier, than when he said they had whit Alaika. But to be fair, Alaika really wasn't that nice to them, Chatan seemed to be nicer.

"Chatan is a shapeshifter who can take the form of a peregrine falcon. He teaches saf, survival and fight. Come on."

Achak followed Annawan into a sort of a hall where already students were waiting. When Achak and Annawan entered the hall, students stopped talking, other ones just gave them a mistrustful look, well at least Achak. Then, after a few moments, they all started talking again. Adahy, Adam and Dexter came to them, as soon as the other students started again with their conversation.

"Hey guys!", Dex called. "Do you know what we're doing here?"

"Well…", Annawan started. "No, I don't really know. The only thing I know is that you… we learn how to survive, camouflage and fight… funny that camouflage isn't in the name of the subjects.", he added.

Adahy opened his mouth to explain what they were doing, in saf, when a falcon flew through the doors into the room, transformed in the middle of them all into a human. Chatan looked at the students with a grin, before he said: "Well, well, well…", he said and looked at the two werewolves. "So, you all noticed that Annawan is here together with his friend Achak. And since I've seen you all in the corridor when the two woke up and all that…"

"Achak, please be a little patient with him. That is his usual way, he's a falcon and doesn't like it when you stay focused on one thing for too long", Annawan whispered towards Achak. Achak nodded with a sassy grin. "But now we have survival and fight. But unfortunately, we must stay inside for today, because Achak and Annawan are getting hunted by Julia La Lune the werewolf hunter. That is the reason we must stay inside… except we go outside and practice, in… groups of four."

Achak leaned to Annawan and whispered: "I like him, he doesn't obey the rules. Even though he is headmaster." Now it was on Annawan to grin and nodded. The shapeshifter looked at the two werewolves and grinned slightly towards them. The students began to whisper, others looked at Achak and at Annawan, until Chatan clapped his hands and said: "So then come on, we have to hurry if you want to have a real situation to practice."

The students all split up in groups of four, in each group it should have at least one which – or wizard – and one shapeshifter. Achak and Annawan just stayed together, so that they would be in a group. In the end the only ones left over were Achak, Annawan, Adahy and a wizard boy with short black hair and black eyes.

"Well, I guess we're a team", Adahy said to Achak and Annawan. "Achak this" (he pointed towards the boy with the black hair and eyes) "is Karl. He is one of the best students in our class... well at least of the witches and wizards. And as long the class isn't saf."

Karl just nodded and said then: "Come on, if we only have one hour then we should get started with building a camp."

The other boys nodded, and so they went outside. But not before Achak and Annawan went to their room, to change. When they were back by their team Achak wore pants made of leather and the necklace of his sister. And Annawan was also wearing pants out of leather, a shirt out of wool and sandals.

"Ok now let's go! We have to hurry if we want to be the first ones!", Karl said quickly. So, they ran into the forest, Achak and Annawan had experience with living and surviving in the forest. In their old leather clothes, they felt more comfortable than human clothes.

"Ok, first we have to find food...", Karl started, but Achak interrupted. "Sorry to interrupt, but you guys have no idea how to survive outside, in the wild. Annawan and I do."

"Yeah, and what do you want to say with that, werewolf?" Karl sounded mad, but why? Maybe because he thinks he's the best at everything, he also has to be the best by surviving? Whatever, he thought and said calmly to Karl:

"Look, if you don't learn to work in a team without you being the alpha, it won't last long till you get caught, or something like that. So, we've only got...ahm...", Achak looked at the stand of the sun. He had enough practice to tell where the sun will stand after an hour. "...about fifty minutes left, and I want to enjoy the sun, and the fresh air, so come on." Annawan already followed Achak and so did Adahy and Adam, while Karl was speaking some curses and then following the group.

In the forest Adahy asked Annawan what to do first, but instead of answering, he looked at Achak. "What do you think? You've been living alone for quite some time. About a year, right?" Achak nodded before thinking what to do and why Annawan put him in charge. Even if he had more experience than Annawan, Annawan was the Alpha. In his old pack Achak had, kind of a beta roll, but never an alpha.

"But Annawan...", Achak started, but Annawan gave him a look that made Achak understand. As alpha Annawan put Achak in charge. To other beings something like that would make sense, but to a werewolf it did. Achak nodded and started thinking.

"Okay Annawan and Adahy go and find water and food, and Karl comes with me to find a place for our camp." The others all nodded and did what Achak said.

"I think I found something", Adahy said after some time searching. "I found a good place, it has a few trees, and it is near to a clearing."

Achak nodded towards his friend, and soon also Annawan and Adahy came back and said that there was a little creek nearby. "Alright then, now we've got to build five sleeping places."

Without words they all started by searching for a long stick, holding it at a tree trunk, then they had to look that the person for which the place was had enough space to lie and sit and then they only had to cover the stick, and the sticks that were leaning on the side, with leaves. And that they made five times, and finished just in time, when Chatan came to check.

"Good work, you guys. Whose idea was it, to do it like that?"

Before anyone could answer Karl said: "Achak. It was Achaks idea."

"Well done Achak. Like that, you save time in building and breaking the camp again after the night, and exactly that you have to do now and then return to the school." Chatan transformed into a falcon and flew away.

The days passed fast, but with every day Achak and Annawan grew more and more inpatient. They were stuck inside the school and could not go out. And that was frustrating, especially for werewolves which grew up in the mountains or the forest, where they were free and did not have to obey anyone, except of course the alpha of the pack. But the point was that the two missed the forest. So, after they have been looked up for a week, they both decided to go out in the night. As werewolves it will be difficult to see them because of their black fur.

Achak thought of the incoming night. What would they do? What will happen? Did Julia La Lune find out where he and Annawan were? As he thought of La Lune, Achak suddenly got pulled right back to the night when she and other humans attacked his pack. He got pulled right to the place where he was standing, when one of the humans was aiming, with his fire breathing stick, towards him, when Hakan, his big brother in form of a werewolf with flaming-red fur, jumped right in front of Achak to protect him of a shot. Achak could feel the stripe shots that hit him, and the burning pain he felt. He felt the burning pain in his chest when he returned after the fight, only to see his family and friends dead on the ground...

A knocking on the door of his room pulled Achak back to the present. He didn't notice the tears in his eyes as he said with a hoarse voice: "Come in." Annawan stepped into the room. He too had signs of sorrow, but Annawan was better in hiding his feelings.

"Well, ready?", Annawan asked and Achak nodded while he was wiping his tears away. Annawan looked at his younger friend before turning into a great wolf with black fur and orange-red glowing eyes. Achaks mood improved right away when he was once again in his familiar wolf form. He followed Annawan outside where the moon shined on his black fur. Achak felt home for a short time. Home, in the mountains where the moon always shined on his black fur and made his eyes glow in an amber-golden color. In the forest, wher9e he could run as long as he wanted, could hunt small rabbits or little birds. In his old territory and with his pack. His parents. His brothers. His sister. While the moon was shining, he suddenly felt a stabbing pain in his chest that he did not feel that hard for nearly a year now. The pain was like sharp claws ripping at his chest, like...

Annawan began to howl. Achak got free from his emotions for a second before he dived right in again and sang with Annawan. They switched with singing. Achak sang a verse and Annawan sang a verse, while they sang the refrain together.

*So, here I am without any hope,*
*Just with questions about the future, about the present,*
*about the past,*
*With grief that ties around me like a strong rope,*
*It is so strong that I just can't get out so fast.*
*I'm losing hope of ever finding you,*
*And we all got separated from each other,*
*I tried to find you but without any luck or a clue,*
*And now I know that I miss my brothers, my father, and*
*my mother.*

*We both lost our family,*
*But we must try to find the source of our pain.*
*Even though, that would not be that easily*
*We must try even if it is in vain.*
*Our names mean spirit and Chief.*
*Chief, for the orange-red glowing eyes,*
*For the ability to stay an unseen thief*
*To be very good to decide, how to disguise.*
*Spirit, for being wild,*
*For also being free,*
*I was always running wild,*
*And just being who I am supposed to be.*

*Well, who would have thought,*
*That the werewolf numbers soon will drop from*
*thousands to naught?*
*The werewolf hunters seem to be winning,*
*but we must stand our ground from the very beginning!*
*My old home, my clan has been destroyed,*
*I start to get a bit annoyed!*
*The La Lunes are a real bane,*
*Their existence has only caused a lot of pain.*

*"Right?"*
*"Yes!"*

*We both lost our family,*

But we must try to find the source of our pain.
Even though, that would not be that easily
We must try even if it is in vain.
Our names mean spirit and chief.
Chief, for the orange-red glowing eyes,
For the ability to stay an unseen thief
To be very good to decide, how to disguise.
Spirit, for being wild,
For also being free,
I was always running wild,
And just being who I am supposed to be.

And now we must find your sister!
I really hope to find her!
That she is still alive...
Believe me, we will find her before you can count to
forty-five!
Don't forget that hope will die at last!
You are right, but the ground to find her is too vast!
But I trust you my friend, but I can't go alone...
Don't worry I'll assist you to the bone!
I'll come with you all the way to the way until you find
her!
Thank you, I hope I will find Mal my sister!

We both lost our family,
But we must try to find the source of our pain.
Even though, that would not be that

*We must try even if it is in vain.*
*Our names mean spirit and Chief.*
*Chief, for the orange-red glowing eyes,*
*For the ability to stay an unseen thief*
*To be very good to decide, how to disguise.*
*Spirit, for being wild,*
*For also being free,*
*I was always running wild,*
*And just being who I am supposed to be.*
*Who I was supposed to be!*
*Who we are supposed to be!!*

The last verse of their song, the two wolves were howling while switching with singing. When they were finished the two wolves looked at each other, before they transformed back into humans, both wearing their "human-clothes".

"You know...", Annawan began before he was interrupted by a shot that came out of the bushes but missed the two friends by a tree length. Achak and Annawan both got frightened by the loud bang and ran away into the forest. But after a while of running Achak could hear another shot and Annawan howling. Achak stopped and looked at his friend. But before he could look at the place where Annawan got shot there was another bang and a stinging pain in Achaks left shoulder. Footsteps and voices. And then everything went black...

# Chapter 7

"... do with the two werewolves? Kill them?"

"Oh, no not yet! We first must weaken them tonight is a full moon night, so we should have no problem tomorrow. Wildmoons are more sensitive to the full moon or silver than other werewolves..."

Achak could hear voices. One was a very familiar female voice, the other one he never heard before. But then he heard another familiar voice, one he was glad to hear.

"Achak...?"

Annawan. He was whispering and his voice did not sound well.

"Annawan?"

Achak tried to move but stopped as he felt a stinging, familiar pain. Silver. Achak looked up and saw silver bars. They were in a cage made of silver!

"Great! We're in a silver-cage!", Achak said and Annawan nodded weakly. Achak knew why, because also he felt weak. It seemed like the full moon would soon rise, and then they would turn into werewolves and had no control over their mind or actions.

"Annawan? I have a question", Achak asked.

"Yes?"

"Do you know why we can transform into normal wolves – and werewolves – at daylight and are still sane, but when the full moon rises, we lose control of ourselves?"

"… Well not really, I think Alaika could have an answer, but I've been asking her for a very long time. Unfortunately, no one ever knew the answer, so I stopped asking."

Achak wanted to say something but got interrupted by Julia La Lune, who now realized that the two woke up.

"So, you finally woke up? Good." She looked at Achak before she grinned and said: "Oh yes, I remember you. How's mummy and daddy? And your brothers?" Achak growled and showed his teeth as he heard how the werewolf-hunter talked about his family. "And your sister…?" That was enough! He suddenly jumped at the La Lune while transforming into a wolf in the jump. He attacked so fast and so surprisingly that the woman could react fast enough. Achak bite her in the arm and drag her nearer to the cage so he would not get burned any longer (he was so near the bars that he got burned in the face). La Lune screamed and soon two men came to help her out of the grip of the great black wolf. The eyes of the wolf were glowing furiously and full of pain. Annawan was just next to the furious wolf but could not do anything because one of the men, one with very short hair and cold blue eyes, was holding him back, so he could not go help his younger friend, while he pressed Annawan with the back against the bars. Annawan yelled, causing the younger wolf to lose his focus for a second before biting even harder, so hard that he could taste the blood of the woman. The wolf did not like the taste of the blood that was running down the arm of the hunter. Even though Achak did not like the taste he kept biting, this woman had killed not only his father, but also his mother, brothers and maybe even Mai, his sister. He wanted to hurt her so badly he could. Achak was so lost in his thoughts that he did not notice the second man, a tall one with blond hair, black eyes and several paintings on his arms (tattoos, how the humans called it), had sneaked *into* the cage and came from the back towards Achak. Annawan wanted to warn his mate, but the man that was holding him put his hand onto his mouth so that the werewolf could not warn his mate. Then Achak sensed the other man behind him but it was too late. The man pushed Achak against the silver bars so that he burned himself and yelled. When he yelled, he had his mouth open wide enough for the werewolf-hunter to pull her arm out, and that she did. As Achak stepped back from the bars the man behind him in the cage pressed him against the bars again so the wolf got burned very badly. Julia La Lune then came with muzzles made of silver. She gave them the man in the cage which put the muzzle on Achak. The silver was burning on his wolf-snout and Achak saw how the men forced Annawan to his wolf form so they could put the muzzle on him as well.

Achak could see how the silver was burning into the flesh of his friend and walked to him.

"I'm sorry... I... I was so angry at her for mentioning my family and..."

"It's okay mate. I think she would have put these muzzles on us at the latest tonight and then it would have been even worse", Annawan didn't sound upset so that Achak believed him, that he wasn't mad at him. But he could see the pain in the eyes of the friend as he spoke. The muzzles were pretty small so that they actually touched the snouts of the two wolves. Also, Achak could feel the burning, why by the seven mountain pikes did he attack La Lune? Because you still did not come over the deaths of your pack and family including your sister, a voice said. A voice that sounded familiar. His brother Hakan! Hakan, he asked in thought. *What do you mean?* Achak felt his brother smiling before he answered: *Tonight, you must sleep and rest. Then I will answer your questions.* With these words Hakans present vanished. Achak started to worry. Sleep on a full moon? That was rare. Normally a werewolf is awake when the full moon shines on their fur. But maybe he could sleep if the moon cannot shine into their cage? Well, guess he just must find out.

Finally, the full moon was rising. Achak felt how his body began to change and how he grew bigger until he was nearly double so big as a wolf. His snout was hurting badly because of the muzzle. But he was right, the moon was not shining in the cage and he felt... peaceful. He knew that tonight, he could sleep. And as soon as the transformation ended, he laid down, closed his eyes and fell asleep.

In his dream, he was in the mountains again. The full moon was shining on a group of people. A man was standing on a big rock. The man had sand-blond hair and orange-yellow eyes, at least in human form. Next to the man there was a woman with withe-blond hair and yellow-golden eyes. And standing right behind them there were four children. The biggest had fire red hair, green eyes and a scar on his cheek that was formed in a cross. Right next to the red-haired boy there was another boy, but with rusty brown hair and foxy orange-brown eyes. The next child was no boy, but a girl with chin long, brown hair (which looked black in the dark) and sparkling green eyes. And right next that girl there was a boy. A boy with chin long, night black hair and amber-brown eyes.

Achak stepped a little closer, he recognized them at once. His family! The man was his father Tocho and the woman his mother Tala. The boy with fire-red hair was Hakan, and the one with rusty-brown hair and the foxy looking eyes was Tokala! And the girl... his twin sister, Mai. The look of his family like this, still alive and not in panic, was so painful that Achak felt as if there were sharp claws and teeth ripping on his heart. Only when he looked at them did he realize how long they have been torn apart. How much he missed them. He looked at his family who had just transformed into werewolves. His father was a great sand-brown werewolf with glowing red eyes. A withe werewolf with brown ears and red glomming eyes was standing next to Tocho. That was his mother, Tala. The werewolf with red like fur and glowing green eyes was Hakan. He was looking way better than before he died. Hakan began to play with another werewolf. Tokala, with rusty-brown fur and foxy orange-brown eyes that were glowing in a sly and cunning way. Achak looked to the two black werewolves that were playing together and with some other werewolves. The black one with withe ears, claws, paws, and green eyes was Mai. Her fur was actually dark brown but because the moon was not shining on her, the difference between black and dark brown was hard to tell. The other werewolf that was completely black and had amber-glowing eyes, was himself. Achak. Achak looked at his sister, she had dark-brown hair as human and dark-brown fur as werewolf, but because of the dark that did not really matter. His family was still alive. But then the truth ran over him like an elk. His family was dead. Killed by werewolf-hunters. Humans! And are now members of the moon-clan.

Achak knew that the scenes before him were just moments before the hunters discovered their lair. The hideout of the dark mountain pack. And then he saw the fight. How humans jumped out of bushes or behind rocks and started to shoot at the werewolves. Achak looked for Mai and saw her how she got shot in the back and collapsed. Achak wanted to look a little longer, after all she somehow managed to walk away. But he got distracted by his dad. Tocho was fighting against three humans. Two men and one woman. Julia La Lune and the two guys who put the muzzles on him and Annawan! Achak felt anger growing in his chest. Julia La Lune killed his father! She was at fault because he did not have a family. Not only did she lead the attack, but she also killed his father!

Achak heard a loud yell and got distracted. That yell was so familiar. He looked to the place where the pups were hiding and saw Hakan. How he jumped in front of his youngest brother and got shot, right in the chest!

"No! Hakan", Achak heard himself howl. "Hakan!" His brother looked at him for a moment and tried to speak. "Go. Please go…"

"No. I… I can't leave you all here…"

"It will be fine… But…", Hakans eyes started to lose their shine. "… if no one stands up to Julia it is the end of our kind… Now, please go and hide…"

"No! I can't just leave the pack...!"
Hakan coughed, looked his brother in the eyes and asked him to go away. And then Hakan closed his eyes and moved                          no                          more.
Achak saw how he shook his head and remembered that he did not want to flee. But then he heard a shot, this one even hit Achak and everything went dark.

"Don't let the sorrow guide you." Achak heard a voice. The voice was so strange and yet so familiar. He opened his eyes. He was still dreaming. He was still in the mountains. But the mountains looked different. They were clean and looked, as if no one ever lived here or even fought. And then Achak noticed the spirits. A few of them looked familiar. He saw a werewolf with sand-brown fur, one with withe fur and brown ears, one had fire red fur and another one had rusty-brown fur. His family! But then other werewolves, who he never saw before in his life, appeared. And yet, he knew them. He knew them all. A werewolf with fur that made a look as if it were burning stood next to another one who looked nearly the same, except that the eyes were not glowing in a gras-green, but in a fiery orange. Those must be the fire-twins. Atsila and Rowtag. Next to them there was a werewolf with fur as grey as the mountains, and eyes that were shining in a silver blue. Acaraho. Rowtag took a step forward and looked at Achak. The eyes of the fire-good were gras-green, but still there was a little flame in them that seemed as if it would burn for eternity.

"Hello, Achak", Atsila said softly. Achak bowed his head in front of her. When he raised his head again, Atsila spoke and said: "We came to tell you something." Atsila fell silent. Achak nodded to show that he was listening, Atsila waited before she spoke.

"You found the diary of Angeni. In the diary she wrote about our prophecy about the wild moon werewolves. Now's the time. Find that prophecy and find the three werewolves of the prophecy."

"But... where is the prophecy? And... did you say *three* werewolves? There are more werewolves that survived Julia La Lune?" Achak was suddenly filled with hope. If the prophecy was about three werewolves, and since his sister was not among the spirits... Could it be that Mai was still alive?

"The prophecy is closer than you think, Achak", Angeni answered the question about the prophecy, but the question about the three werewolves she did not answer. Atsila turned around and stepped to her brother. Rowtag stepped closer to the younger werewolf, looked at him, his eyes were burning-orange and in his eyes, there was a flame that seemed to burn for eternity. Rowtag said, in a deep and soft voice:

"Hey Achak. I wanted to say that I am sorry about your family. I know how you feel."

"Really", Achak asked. Rowtag nodded, and for a second the flame seemed to go out, but it went right on again.

"Yes. Atsila died before me. She was killed by the couple Sarah and Sam La Lune, while hunting. I was devastated and I felt the same way as Shiriki when Jacy got shot, I know it is a strange way to compare but I think that Shiriki is the closest to how I felt. Atsila and I were twins. Shiriki and Jacy were twins. And you and Mai are twins. I know how you feel."

He gave Achak a sad look, which didn't really go with his burning fur. The twins vanished and Acaraho now looked at Achak. The silver-grey eyes were glowing. Acaraho first watched Achak before he began to speak:

"So, so, the Spirit Achak. Descendant of Angeni", he paused. "How's Annawan? And how are you?"

"… I think we're fine. Except maybe the muzzles", Achak answered. Acaraho looked at Achak for a minute before he spoke.

"Muzzles? What did La Lune do", the voice of the werewolf-god was furious. Achak suddenly felt that all the gods had a connection to the La Lunes. "That filthy rat!" Achak looked at Acaraho. Did he know the La Lunes? Personally? Maybe even the first one? Achak wanted to ask Acaraho what he meant but before he could do so, the fire twins and Acaraho disappeared. The only ones who were still here was his family.

"What did Acaraho...?", Achak could not finish, instead he suddenly woke up. Mighty full moon, he thought. But he quickly forgot his anger as he saw why he woke up.

# Chapter 8

Achak woke up and the first thing that happened was a stinging pain. Not only on his snout, but also in his leg, and most of all in his back. He looked around. Julia La Lune was standing right next to him and was looking at Annawan. Achak looked at Annawan, he was the one who woke him up. And Achak saw why. With a silver rope Julia La Lune had tied his legs together. Achak saw that Annawan was fighting with himself, but why? Julia did not seem to notice that the second werewolf woke up. Instead, she focused on Annawan.

"After all these years, all the generations of La Lunes succeed! The end of the werewolves is here. Oh, don't look at me like that", she added as she saw how Annawan was looking. Also, Achak could see now why his friend was fighting with himself. So, he will not burst into tears. The silver ropes were burning into his flesh, and Achak knew how that must feel. "You must have known that this day would come. And with you and your pathetic little friend, I destroy the only creature that could be in my way. In two days, I will kill you and your friend, in front of my village. In front of reporters and my family will be rich!" Achak looked at Annawan, who noticed him. Annawan seemed to know what Achak would do because he shook his head. But Achak ignored his friend and began to sneak up on La Lune. Annawan gave up on trying to convince Achak not to do that, but still looked at him.

Achak was now right behind the woman who killed his father. He jumped at her, she screamed and wanted to grab the werewolf to tie him up, but Achak was faster. He leaped away from her and to Annawan. He was standing by his friend and began to growl. It did not look that terrifying with a muzzle but still showed the effect. Achak was so furious that he did not even care about the burning in his back, in his legs and on his snout. He just stood over his friend, ready to protect him. Annawan tried to get up on his feet but fell again. Julia went out and gave Achak a look that surely meant nothing good. When she was gone Achak turned around to Annawan, who didn't look that well.

"Are you okay pal?"

"Nope. Not really no. Were you sleeping? On a full moon?"

"... Yes...", Achak started but Annawan interrupted.

"What did you dream about?" Annawan sounded excited

"Well, first I was in the mountains again. During the fight. Then suddenly my family, the fire twins and Acaraho appeared. Atsila told me about a prophecy... you remember Angenis' diary?" Annawan nodded, slowly and Achak continued: "Well apparently Atsila was talking about that prophecy. She said that I must find the three werewolves of the prophecy and…"

"*Three?* Did you say three? There are other werewolves that survived?"

"That was just what I asked, but she did not answer. She said the prophecy is nearer than I think. Do you know what that could mean?"

"No, I'm afraid not, but Maybe…?"

Annawan got interrupted, Julia La Lune was reading aloud from a scroll:

"… Great-great-great-great grandson of Angeni. And great-great-great-great grandson of Catori. Spirit and Chief, the last wildmoons and half-brothers. Son of Thunder and Wolf. 12 shall he be when the youngest son of Puma and Wolf shall be born. The sister of Spirit shall be named Coyote and help them on their way to end the La Lunes…"

Achak couldn't listen anymore. That was the prophecy, no doubt! But what was the rest? Mouse head, why did I stop listening, he asked himself. Maybe there was more information about the prophecy and of the werewolves in it. Werewolf prophecies are known to be very precise, sometimes even the names of the werewolf appear! He needed that prophecy! But… how should he get it?

Maybe...? No! That is a bit too risky even for his taste. But, how else...?

"Achak? Did you hear that?" Annawan looked at Achak, while he nodded. Annawan was thinking the same thing. "How do we get it", Annawan asked one heartbeat after Achak nodded.

"Hmm... I don't know, but... I've got an idea... but it's risky", he added. Annawan grinned and said: "I should be used to it."

"Why that?"

"My little brothers and sisters were always playing, and I had to look for them and make sure they'll see the next full moon. They loved risky things and were little foxes. But I must admit that they got really talented in getting into trouble and surviving." Annawan smiled sadly, Achak wanted to know more and asked:

"What were their names?"

"Do you also want to know my older siblings? I've got plenty you know." Achak laughed and said yes.

"Okay, my oldest brother was called Falconwing. He was 24 when he died, and he had yellow eyes with a thin black circle around them, that's why they called him Falconeye, wing just came because he had a friend who was falcon and died just moments after I was born. He had a broken wing, and to honor the falcon my clan changed Falconeye, to Falconwing." Annawan paused for a moment and seemed to lose himself in memories before he snapped out of it and continued: "Then, my sister Thunderhair. She was only one year younger than Falconwing and got her name because there was a violent thunderstorm when she was born and when she got hair it looked a bit like clouds right before a storm. My brothers Fast Lightning and Lightning Night were twins. I think I don't have to explain where they got their names of, do I?"

"No you don't, but I got a question."

"Yeah?"

"Did all your clan members have names like that?"

"No, only a few. Others had names just like you and me. But I guess more than half of them had such names, mostly with lightning or thunder." Annawan grinned before he continued: "Now, my little brothers Abey and Abeytu were twins and my little sister Amadahy and her twin brother Akando also. And then my youngest sibling was my brother Devaki..."

"I got it!"

"What?"

"An idea."

Annawans face lit up and with a nod he encouraged him to speak.

"Okay, first we must get rid of these muzzles, it will burn but... rather burn myself by getting rid of these things, than die in front of dozens of humans." Annawan nodded and Achak continued. "Then we have to wait. When Julia comes, I'll bite her – again – and you have to, somehow, get rid of her two 'betas'. When they aren't much of a danger we have to get out of here, if there is no other way, we have to break this cage, even if we will burn ourselves. When we get outside, we must go back to the school." Achak looked at his friend, that one looked rather pensive.

"You know that that is extremely reckless, risky and dangerous?"

Achak got unsure and slowly said "Well... yeah ... yes."

Annawan started grinning before he said:

"I'm in."

# Chapter 9

"Alright. Annawan, you know what to do."

"Yes."

It was night again and Achak and Annawan wanted to escape. Now. Okay, step one, perhaps the most difficult one, get rid of the muzzles without drawing attention. So, after a while Achak slowly moved one of his paws towards the muzzle (he and Annawan were still in wolf form). Just as his paw touched the silver, Achak felt a burning pain. It was as if he was holding his paw into fire. But he did not stop, he tried to get the damn thing of. For a second, he also saw Annawan, also he seemed to be fighting with the burning pain of the silver. Then, finally Achak succeeded and the muzzle flew to the ground. Also, Annawan seemed successful, for a short time Achak was frightened when he saw Annawans face, It was covered in burnings.

"Well then, let's do this", Annawan said. Achak nodded as answer, now they had to wait for the blond La Lune. They did not have to wait long, as they heard steps. And then, only a few moments later Achak saw Julia La Lune. She looked as if she just found out that there were more werewolves that she could hunt.

"Seems like I'm a very lucky woman. The town said that they are ready to see you tomorrow at dawn."

Achak would have bitten her with or without plan when she said that. But this time he bites even heather than he agreed with Annawan, and Achak did not really care at that moment. Because he saw a fur on the wall. The fur looked sand brown and was so familiar, the only thing different about it was that, usually there were red eyes glowing, but here they seemed dark and empty. It was the fur of his father Tocho. Achak was so furious that he started to rip the arm open, so the woman could not use it for the next moons. As she yelled, Achak let go of her. Annawan had already hurt one of the men badly and the other one was kneeling next to his partner. Achaks friend saw him and stepped out of the cage. They both started running, they did not know where, but at least away from La Lune!

"How bad did you hurt her?", Annawan asked, while running.

"I hope so badly that she cannot use her arm for the rest of her life!"

The two wolves passed more than just one room. But suddenly Annawan stopped.

"Hey, look." Annawan nodded towards a scroll that said:

*The end of the La Lunes and werewolves*

"Didn't we look for a prophecy? Well, guess that's it", Annawan finished.

"Quick, we need to get that scroll and flee!"

Annawan rushed to the scroll, took it with his mouth and went back to his friend. He unrolled it and read loud:

*Great-great-great-great grandson of Angeni.*

*And great-great-great-great grandson of Catori.*

*Spirit and Chief, the last wildmoons and half-brothers. Son of Thunder and Wolf. 6 shall he be when the youngest son of Puma and Wolf shall be born. The sister of Spirit shall be named Coyote and help them on their way to end the La Lunes.*

*Both will be black haired and have brown eyes. But Spirit will have black fur, while Chief has got light-brown fur, though, black haired.*

*But still, both will take loss and suffer. And yet they will be heroes and gods in the end.*

*Good luck Achak and Annawan*

"Did I get that right?", Achak asked. "We are the ones? The ones to end the La Lunes. Oh, holy full moon how are we going to do that? And...?"

Annawan just wanted to answer, as they both could hear steps and voices. The two wolves began to run, the scroll still in Annawans mouth. But suddenly Julia was standing right in front of them, her right arm covered in blood and slashed. In both hands she had knives. Before even one of the two wolves knew what, they should do, Julia already had raised her knives and as she swung the knives, she somehow managed to cut them both. Achak and Annawan both yelled and when La Lune was distracted by her own victory they ran. Achak did not know where to, just away.

After they brought enough distance between them and the werewolf-hunter the two stopped, to look at each other. When Achak looked at Annawan he frightened at first. His friend was burned quite hard in the face. As humans the scars would be obvious. Now, as a wolf, the scars over lips and cheek were not that obvious, the only one who would be, is the one that was still bleeding. The one over the right eye, that started just inches before his eye and ended on his right scar free cheek.

But also, Annawan looked at Achaks eye for a long time. Achak knew why, Julia also cut him in the face. Not over the right eye like Annawan, but the left eye.

"So, back to the prophecy", Achak said. Werewolf prophecies were always quite precise so that it would not take too long to find out what they mean. And that one was obvious.

"We both are the ones to end the La Lunes. And we'll be gods in the end? Oh yeah, why not? After all we are the only werewolves left, so...", Achak stopped because Annawan suddenly rose his head. Now also Achak heard the voice of Julia La Lune. Achak looked at Annawan and they both began to run. But where to? Where can they escape?

*You are close Achak*, a voice whispered. It was Hakan. Then, the voice of Rowtag joined, left and then right and *you will see the moon shine again.*

"We need to turn left and then right!", Achak said to Annawan.

"How do you know that?"

"My brother and Rowtag told me!"

Annawan nodded and they both ran together, turned left and then right. By the door Annawan stood on his hind legs and opened it with his front paw. And when the door was open, the two ran out as fast as they could heading towards the forest.

When they were finally in the forest, the two stopped, and transformed again into humans.

Annawans face was full of scars yet, the most obvious scar was the one that was still bleeding. Achak looked at his half-brother which looked back at him.

"Okay, now, back to the school." Achak agreed and they both walked in the direction where the moon usually is at his highest point. In the forest, Achak noticed that Annawan was limping. He ignored his own pain even though he was a bit more sensitive to silver.

"So, Achak. We are half-brothers, are the last wildmoons, the ones to end the La Lunes and what do I know what else…", Annawan started. Achak smiled. Annawan was trying to loosen up the mood. With success.

"Seems so."

The two walked without stopping. The chances that Julia will find the war was too big, even for Achak it was too dangerous.

The next night Annawan said that they were almost by the Nahuelschool. Achak was glad to hear that, because the burnings that came from the silver didn't heal the way normal wounds do. Normal wounds would have been closed by now, but these silver wounds were bleeding and bleeding. Thanks to Annawan, he and Achak did not lose that much blood yet. Annawan had a few leather straps and found some yarrow to stop the bleeding. The yarrow did help, but still they were bleeding, at least not that hard. And with the leather straps, Annawan bandaged the worst and most bleeding wounds so they would make it back with most of their blood.

"We're almost there", Annawan said to Achak. And yes. They could see the building. And outside Kai was standing. Where were you two?" Kai sounded a little angry, but when they told him what happened he just nodded and called the squirrel siblings. When they came, Achak and Annawan shook their heads saying that they were all right. The twins and Kai could not disagree, so they just turned around and went back inside. The werewolves followed them.

"Okay, what's next?" Achak asked Annawan. They returned to the school two days ago and started again with class. Today they already had saf and they will have history.

Achak and Annawan stepped into the classroom and took a seat. Annawan was behind Achak and in the middle of Dex and Karl, while Achak was sitting in between Adahy and Adam. And then the teacher stepped in. It was the wizard Jack. He was a tall wizard with with-blond hair and blue eyes.

"Al right class. Today we will learn how the wizards, the shapeshifters, the werewolves, and the humans got along thru time. I know that we have not discussed their origins yet, but that will come soon. So, does someone know, or believes to know, how these four beings got along?"

Achak looked around, a few students were holding up their hands. Also, Adahy on his left, and Adam on his right seemed to know a few things. Jack looked at a girl with bushy curled brown hair and said:

"Yes, Anabel?"

"Well, I do know that witches and wizards were hunted, that was about 600 years ago. I think... and if the humans actually caught a witch, she was burned."

Achak, never heard of something like that, but to be fair, he never wanted to have much contact with humans... and never really had.

"That is correct. But why? How did humans find out that some of us have magical powers?"

No one answered. So, Jack explained.

"You see, we cannot tell that exactly. But a lot of us think that a few witches and wizards just were not careful enough. And so, humans discovered our magical powers. What about the shapeshifters?"

Adahy and Adam were holding their hands wide up into the air. Jack smiled and said:

"Yes, Adahy? Adam?"

The two shapeshifters looked at each other and Adahy began to speak.

"The humans never really found out about us, so we didn't have much trouble with them..."

"... but there were humans that knew of us. They lived with nature and were different from the humans of today. These humans hunted for food, not for sports. They had gods and respected nature. There are stories that they also were the first shapeshifters, but we don't really know", Adam finished. Jack nodded and added:

"Some of the Shapeshifters even say that that was the start of the werewolves too. When these humans discovered a way to transform into animals. Some of them found a way to change permanently to an animal. But when they did that with wolves, they still were bigger and faster than normal wolves.

And after being like that for centuries, a young wizard crossed paths with such a pack. He was terrified, for he never saw such big wolves before. So, he casted a spell that should transform them to humans. But because he did not know what power the moon had on these wolves, he could not know that when the moon's power is the strongest, and that's by full moon, they would transform back to wolves. How they developed, we will discuss another time.

But back to the actual topic, maybe one of our werewolves can answer the question?"

Achak looked back at Annawan. His half-brother looked ill. His eyes were cheerless, and Achak noticed dark rings under his eyes. Achak had to admit that also he was not feeling very good, but he could swear that he looked better than Annawan. Annawan looked at Jack before he spoke:

"Humans and werewolves never really got along. And since the La Lunes discovered our existence, we were at war with humans ever since and retreated into the mountains, the forests, the prairies, the deserts, jungles, the tundra. Or we were traveling from one place to another."

Jack nodded with a slight smile, looked on his watch and said that they could go.

When Achak stood up he felt a hard burning, in his back, in his legs. Everywhere. He forced himself to walk out. Annawan waited, together with Adam, Adahy, Dex and Karl. Achak went to his friends and his half-brother, so that they could go to their next class together. Which would be human study. But suddenly he felt something warm running down his face. Next, he heard screams of girls and all the students around them. He looked at Annawan. The wound of his right eye seemed to have opened, also all other scars in his face were bleeding. But Achak only saw it for a heartbeat. Annawan collapsed and stayed lying on the ground. Also, Achak felt the warm blood running down his cheek. His legs, arms, back. Everything was hurting. He collapsed to the ground. And everything went black.

# Chapter 10

Achak woke up. He was in a bed. He looked to the side and saw Annawan looking at him. He had bandages all over his body. Some of them were red, and Achak knew that those must be the wounds because of silver.

Also, he had such bandages. Most of them were red and wet. Then he saw four boys walking towards them. Adahy, Adam, Dexter, and Karl. The four of them came to the two werewolves.

"Phou… you got us shocked guys. We were worried." Adahy spoke and looked at his two friends. Annawan looked up but moaned and laid back down. Achak and the other boys looked at the werewolf of the thunder clan. Before any of the boys could say something, Steffi, and Steve came to their beds to change the bandages of the half-brothers. When they treated Annawan, he gasped painfully and Achak could see that the back of the fellow werewolf was hurt almost as badly as his face.

Annawan noticed the look of Achaks face, smiled and said:

"Don't look at me like a wolf that got attacked by a mouse. It looks ridiculous."

Achak started to laugh and so did the other boys.

"Hold still!" Steffi said to Annawan, who moved a little bit. "I can't treat your wounds properly if you'd just stay still." Steffi disinfected the wounds after cleaning them. Annawan did hold still, until the squirrel-shifter wanted to disinfect the sore back, legs, and arms. Steffi gave him a warning look, and Annawan stayed still.

After she disinfected all wounds of Annawan and Achak, she left, to leave the boys alone.

"All right, who can tell us what happened?" Achak looked at Adahy. "Well, first I have to say that you already looked awful, but we thought it just was because of the silver. But... well... after history class, you started bleeding and Annawan too. In your face, your arms, legs, we all got frightened. You both were bleeding so hard... then Annawan collapsed and you followed."

Achak looked at Annawan, they both looked at each other and Annawan explained to the boys that he was very sensitive to silver, and apparently Achak as well.

"I think it has to do with the fact that we are wildmoons," he added. "There are stories that Jacy and Shiriki were sensitive to silver as well. When they had contact with silver, they would have scars that just suddenly started to bleed." Adam looked at his lynx-friend, and they both looked at their fox and their wizard friends. They all four looked kind of terrified. Achak could imagine why. The look of him and his brother must have been terrifying.

Adam opened his mouth to say something, but before he could do so the doors opened and Kai, Jack and Chatan came in.

"So, how are you both?" Kai asked. Achak felt better but still tired, and most of him was still hurting. But as he looked towards Annawan he knew that they did not both feel the same way.

Annawan had dark rings under his eyes, his face was pale, and he seemed even more tired than Achak himself.

"I'm better, but Annawan... I don't really think that he's okay...", Achak said. Annawan did not seem to hear what Achak just said. Normally he would have said that he was all right and that kind of stuff, but now he just laid himself down again and fell asleep.

It took Annawan a few hours to wake again. Until then it was night, and the teachers and the boys were not in the room anymore.

"So, Achak", Annawan started. "Julia knows our names. And, well I don't really think we can go under humans with our birth names, right?"

"Well yeah, but I don't want to be under humans!" Achak furiously responded. Annawan just looked at his little half-brother. And Achak noticed that Annawan looked better. Healthier. His face was not that pale anymore and his eyes were glowing as if he was a werewolf, but not the alpha-likely red, but in a mixture of his human brown eyes and his normally orange-red eyes when he was a werewolf.

"I know… me neither but we must, we have to blend in. For the shapeshifters and wizards and witches that is easy, but for us werewolves it is not. We must buy new clothes, we need names, human names. You understand what I mean?"

"Yes, I… I actually do."

Achak did understand but it would not be easy. If even Annawan could not fit in – and he was 12 hunting seasons older than Achak – how could he? We just must try, he thought. So now the two were exchanging ideas of what their human names could be, and how they would dress if they ever go to the humans.

"I think Peter would be an excellent name for you Annawan", Achak said to his friend with a grin.

"No way! You know, maybe we should name us after something that will still describe us, you know what I mean?"

Achak nodded, and just in that moment Jack came to see them. He asked how they were and as they responded that they were better and told him about their idea Jack helped them by finding a name.

"Hmm… Peter means stone or rock, well that doesn't fit at all." They were searching for a name for Annawan first and then one for Achak. "Martin? No, a warrior does not really fit either, something that has to do with a leader… hmm. Maybe Stefan, that means crown, or Leo. Leo means lion," Jack added. Annawan was thinking, he could not decide. "You can also take both you know. One as first name and the other one as middle name."

"Oh, okay. Then I will take Leo. My name will be Leo Stefan Thunderbolt. How's that?"

"Perfect."

"Great! My turn! Jack, any suggestions?"

Jack smiled and searched for names:

"So, a first name… Milo doesn't fit you. Not even to your look, at least by my opinion. Anyway, let's keep searching. Aha this one suits you. You are friendly right?" Achak grinned and Annawan replied: "Oh yes he is friendly, if not I don't think we would understand each other."

"Great. Achak how do you like Dakota?"

"Dakota? I like that, it is also a werewolf name, but I like the sound of it. I take Dakota. Dakota Nightsky."

On the next day Annawan and Achaks health dropped again. Their wounds opened and were bleeding hard. Steffi and Steve had to change the bandages every hour. And once after they changed the bandages, and

Annawan was sleeping began Achak to drift away. He could hear Steve talk to Kai.

"I'm sorry Kai, we are doing the best we can. But the wounds always open again. We don't have the knowledge about werewolf species to treat such wounds."

"I understand, maybe we can ask one of them. When they are better, one of them must know something about that."

"Okay, but now we have to let them sleep. They must rest. Especially Annawan. The silver affected him deeply, much more than Achak. I wonder why. They are both werewolves. Both wildmoons. So why is there such a difference?"

Achak thought about it. It was true, Annawan was more sensitive to silver. But why? And he also had more contact with silver than Achak, yet the silver made more damage by Annawan. Achak wanted to stay awake a little longer so he could find the answer, but a feeling of weakness o vercame the young werewolf. He felt that blood was running down his face, but he didn't know what Steffi and Steve did. Because he drifted away, lost sight... and then there was only black.

Achak woke again in the night, also Annawan seemed to be awake. He had a book in his hands and was reading in it.

"Annawan? What is that for a book?"

Annawan raised his head and answered: "Remember the book of Angeni we found?" Achak nodded. "Well, it isn't just a diary. It holds information about us. About werewolves. And it was not written by Angeni or Catori… Here take a look." Annawan gave Achak the book. He was right. Those words and pictures were much older that that one from Angeni or Catori. Even the writing was different. That was amazing! He gave Annawan a look and then read aloud:

"The werewolf's origin is much more complicated than many thinks. We are older than the shapeshifters. Here it is, the story of werewolves:

*The werewolf has his roots in the time the humans called the Stone age. A young non werewolf boy called Malum found out that his brother and many other children of not only his group, but also the group of others, turned into gigantic wolves once a month by full moon. He studied these children until he was a young man. The boy noticed that there were different kinds and looks of the creatures he started to call vir lupus. Those were the first Latin words no one ever knew, and the boy did not want to let others know, for a real language had not existed yet, only names.*

*The boy then once spoke to his brother named lupus. With hand signs he asked his brother: "When did you want to tell me? You change every moon to a wolf?" Lupus was terrified that his brother knew and explained that he could not tell him, because he would fear him. The younger brother of Lupus ensured him that he is not scared and would never tell anyone. Lupus was relieved and invited his brother to meet the other ones, before they all would go and have their own clan with just them. The first clan of werewolves.*

*In the night Malum went with Lupus and got to know other vir Lupi. Lupus warned Malum to stay away from them during the full moon. Malum agreed and went to hide behind bushes. As the moon appeared, the vir Lupi transformed. Malum noticed the different kinds. A few looked terrifying, with no hair, green eyes, tall and sharp claws. Another group was smaller, they had black eyeballs, four tows and walked and stood on their hindlegs. And then there were the wolves that looked completely normal, except maybe that they were bigger, had withe eyes and shorter hindlegs. Other ones had shining eyes, they still had a humanoid shape, their toes and fingers just became sharp claws, and their teeth became like those of a wild dog (at least that's how we describe them).*

*And then there were only five others. His brother Lupus, two other boys and two other girls. They looked like a mix between the other four looks of werewolves. They looked like a normal wolf, but their eyes were glowing in different colors, and they got sharp claws. Malum was a bit scared now but still he stayed to draw the five looks and named them: The one that we know today as European werewolf he named Europae vin Lupi, the Asian werewolf he named Asian vin Lupi. The Lokoti werewolf he called Lokoti vin Lupi, the North American werewolves were named North American vin Lupi and finally, the wildmoon he called Luna feram.*

*Malum stayed with the werewolves for a long time. He even fell in love with a Lokoti werewolf woman. She had black hair and blue eyes as a human, but with withe-brown fur and blue eyes with a bit of yellow as werewolf. Her name was Nix. Together they had children. Noctis was the oldest son, he had black hair and green eyes both as human and as werewolf. Their second son had sand-brown fur and green-blue eyes as werewolf and sand-brown hair with blue eyes as human, Malum and Nix called him Harenae. And their youngest child was a girl that looked just like Nix, and that is why they called her Nix.*

*Now the werewolf-line started. The idea of the names we know today, came from the daughter of Noctis. The werewolves had a perfect life, for the normal humans respected them. But in time the humans wanted more power, they knew about witches, wizards and even came up with stories about shapeshifters. Most afraid they all were of the werewolves, and so a man who managed to kill Acaraho became a hero. And so, did his family. The war between humans and werewolves began.*

*Werewolves began to spread the story that they were as old as the shapeshifters, so no one will ever know how we once had the power and were the connection between humans and animals...*

*Rowtag and Atsila the hot-headed ones*

"That is amazing! We werewolves we got along with humans, thanks to Malum and Lupus! Wow!!"
Achak was amazed. They were older than shapeshifters or wizards and witches!
"Hey Achak, I think we should keep this a secret, don't you?"
"... Hmm. You are right brother... let's don't tell anybody about..." Achak got interrupted by footsteps. Kai and Jack came to them.

"Well, I think we got wonderful news. Especially for you Achak." Achak looked at Annawan. Was it possible that...?

Jack gave him the newspaper of the day. On the front page there was a picture of a girl with dark-brown hair that reached her chin and green eyes. She had a headband. A read one. Or was it grey? Or brown? Never mind! The girl was surrounded by a pack of coyotes and... No way! A lynx was right next to her, and a raven flew over the special group.

Over the photo it stood in fat black letters:

**Boy that lives with animals was caught freeing a dog. He got shot but could flee with a group of coyotes, back into the forest!**

"That is not a boy", Achak yelled, with tears in his eyes. "That's my sister! Mai!" The last sentence he whispered but then said it again: "That's my sister! Mai! She... She's still alive!" Achak laughed in relief. His sister was alive!

"Ha, I thought so", Jack said. Achak was so happy that his sister was still alive that he didn't notice the blood of the scratch over his eye running down his cheek.

"Achak you started to bleed..." Annawan started but Achak interrupted and said:

"Doesn't matter, just a little scratch! What does it matter after all? My sister is alive!"

Annawan had to smile, and so did Kai and Jack. But then Annawans face went serious again and he said to his brother:

"Achak; you don't really have the stupid idea to go and search for your sister, right?" Also, Achaks face went serious, and he responded: "Why not? I have searched for her for over six hunting seasons. And now there is news that she is still alive, you do not seriously accept me just staying here."

"You really have the stupid idea to go and search for her? Look I understand you, but you cannot find her. She could be anywhere!"

"Look Annawan, brother. I am going to find her if it kills me."

Zeitfracht Medien GmbH
Ferdinand-Jühlke-Straße 7
99095 Erfurt, Deutschland
produktsicherheit@kolibri360.de